KING ARTHUR
His Knights
&Their Ladies

Johanna Johnston

SCHOLASTIC INC.
New York Toronto London Auckland Sydney

ISBN 0-590-30007-5 (Student Edition)
ISBN 0-590-30055-5 (Teacher Edition)

12 11 10 9 8   3/9

Printed in the U.S.A.   40

CONTENTS

FOREWORD

Was there ever a real King Arthur? Historians say yes, but not the one of the legends and stories.

Back in the sixth century A.D., after the Romans had quit the British Isles because of their own troubles back home in Italy, Britain became a crazy quilt of little kingdoms, each ruled by its own despotic king or chieftain.

Then, somewhere in the land, a strong chieftain appeared who managed to weld some of the little kingdoms together, repel the advances of Saxon invaders to the south, and make a larger kingdom called England.

There are some scholars who suggest that this chieftain or king was not a Briton but a Roman, Cassius Arturus. But no one knows for sure.

Whoever he was exactly, he was obviously the sort of leader around whom legends cluster. Through the years, and then through the centuries, people told each other stories about Arthur, giving him credit for all sorts of brave deeds, making him the focal figure in any exciting story of war or magic or romance, and changing the background details to make them contemporary and familiar.

About the beginning of the Middle Ages, in the twelfth century, a man named Geoffrey of Monmouth wrote down what he called the history of Arthur. It was a hodgepodge of all the tales and legends that had grown up over the years around the name of Arthur.

Stories about Arthur were also popular in France, and a writer there used him as a hero of a long romance. Other chroniclers had their own variations on the saga, adding anything that seemed dramatic.

Most of these tales were passed on by word of mouth. Only a few were set down in the painstaking, hand-lettered manuscripts of the time.

Then came the invention of movable type. The Bible was the first book to be printed but soon other works were being set in type so that there could be many more copies than manuscripts could provide.

In 1470, soon after this invention, Sir Thomas Malory wrote out the whole Arthurian story once again, changing it, rearranging it, adding bits and pieces from all the versions he had heard, trying to make it as beautiful as he could. He set the story in the early Middle Ages and he was the one who made Arthur the father of chivalry.

Malory's version of the Arthur story, called *Le Morte d'Arthur* became the most famous of all. His is the version on which poets and novelists have based their retellings of the legend through the years since.

This retelling of the old and magical stories is also based on Malory's book, *Le Morte d'Arthur*.

I.

OF THE BIRTH OF ARTHUR

It befell in the days of Uther Pendragon, when he was king of England...

What befell first was love. There was the king, the Pendragon himself, sitting at the great banqueting table, staring at the lady Igraine as if he were under a spell. When she so much as looked his way, he smiled like a dazzled child.

"Please," he stammered, "would you like...can I give you...?" He picked up dishes at random, leaning toward her.

This would all have been very well except that the lady Igraine was already married, to Gorlois, the Duke of Cornwall. She had three fine, nearly grown daughters. More than that, she was a loyal and faithful wife.

She spoke softly to her husband later that night after they had retired to their quarters. "I think, my lord, it would be well if we left this castle very soon. Perhaps even this very night, for I have no wish to be dishonored —let him be King of all England or whoever."

The duke understood her.

3

They gathered their belongings and stole out from the castle at Camelot to ride southward through the night to their own home in Cornwall.

Uther was dumbfounded the next morning when he learned they were gone. He was king. He was Pendragon. Howling, he sent a messenger galloping to Cornwall, summoning the duke and his wife to return at once.

In due time the messenger returned. The Duke of Cornwall had refused to obey the king's summons.

Uther Pendragon stared around at his advisors. "A cause for war?" he cried.

"Oh, aye, my lord." They all nodded and agreed. "Truly a cause for war. March on him at once."

Uther Pendragon was silent for a moment, hooding his eyes. He thought how good it would be to surprise the Duke of Cornwall, finish him off, and then claim Igraine with no one to say him nay. Except—for all his warring—Uther was a decent man. He did not like the idea of ambushing a man so as to steal his wife. He frowned. Then he opened his eyes and looked around at his councilors. "We will send him fair warning," he said.

Another messenger rode off to tell Gorlois to gird himself and lay in provisions because in forty days' time Uther Pendragon was coming.

The duke had two fine castles in Cornwall. One was called Tintagel and one was Terrabil. Tintagel was a splendid, turreted castle built at the shoreline of a little cove that curved in from the English Channel. Terrabil was farther inland and somewhat massive. Gorlois fortified them both and laid in provisions. Then he sent his wife, Igraine, to Tintagel, while he stayed at Terrabil.

Uther counted out the forty days, Igraine's image in

his heart. Then he gathered his knights together and rode south. His army pitched their pavilions before the castle Terrabil and the siege began.

He was not called Pendragon for nothing. His catapults lobbed great stones over the walls of the castle. His archers shot flaming arrows into the embrasures. Fighting men raised ladders against the castle walls and rushed up them.

But the Duke of Cornwall was a good fighting man also and so were his knights. They dumped hot oil and rocks on Uther's men who were climbing the ladders. They sent off flaming arrows of their own and fired rocks.

The siege went on until Uther began to go a little crazy. He felt so ill that he took to his bed. Sir Ulfius, one of his knights, came to him. "Sire, what is it?" he asked. "Is there any way that I can serve?"

"I burn," said Uther. "I burn with anger that I cannot overcome Gorlois." Then his voice became softer and more secret. "I burn with love for the lady Igraine."

"My lord," said Sir Ulfius, "perhaps it is time to seek Merlin."

"Merlin!" said Uther. He had not thought about that clever wizard at all since he had fallen in love. "Merlin," he said again.

"Yes," said Sir Ulfius. "He may be able to remedy your sorrows. Shall I go seek him?"

"Yes," said Uther. "Go now. Go at once."

Sir Ulfius had no idea which way to travel. Merlin might be anywhere and looking like anybody. But he set out bravely.

He had not gone far when a beggar sitting beside the road hailed him and called, "Whom do you seek?"

5

"What is it to you?" said Ulfius, reining his horse.

"Tut, tut," said the beggar. "A civil question deserves a civil answer. However, as it happens, I know whom you seek and you need travel no further." He threw back the hood that half covered his face.

"Merlin?" said Ulfius doubtfully. Sometimes it was hard to tell.

"The same," said the wizard. "I also know why you seek me and I am ready to help King Uther. Under certain conditions."

"I am sure he will agree to anything reasonable, Merlin. He is quite beside himself."

"Ride back to the king. Tell him I will be there soon after you."

Sir Ulfius took his tidings to the king.

"He is coming?" said Uther eagerly. "When? Tomorrow? The day after?"

"Now," said a voice, and there was someone at the opening of the pavilion dressed in long black furs and looking like a Cossack.

"Merlin?" asked Uther.

The strangely dressed creature came in and stood by the king's bed. "Sire," he said, "I know all your heart and I will grant your desires if you swear a certain vow to me."

"You will help me to win Igraine?" asked Uther.

"First you must swear... After you win Igraine, you will have a child by her. When that child is born it shall be delivered to me, to be raised and nourished as I see fit. Do you swear?"

A child? By Igraine? It seemed like a dream to Uther. "I swear it," he said.

And then, what befell next was magic — Merlin's magic.

Late that night, Merlin led Uther to the gate of the castle Tintagel, where the lady Igraine was staying. But as they approached the drawbridge over the moat, the guards could not tell that the two who signaled for the bridge to be lowered were not the Duke of Cornwall and one of his knights. The bridge came down.... The two walked across it. The great gates to the castle courtyard were opened, and the two made their way through the yard and into the castle. Servants hurried with torches to light the way for the man they thought was their duke.

Merlin stayed beside Uther until they came to the doors of the lady's chamber. "Remember," he said, "speak as little as possible and come the moment I call for you in the morning." After that, he turned and left.

Uther opened the doors of the lady Igraine's bed-chamber and went inside. And that night he did have his heart's desire and held the lady in his arms the whole night through.

A little before dawn Merlin came tiptoeing into the room and touched Uther on the shoulder. Uther gave the lady one last kiss and arose and hurried after Merlin, out of the castle and back to his own pavilion.

Then he learned that one of his knights had killed the Duke of Cornwall when he ventured out of the castle Terrabil earlier in the night.

Soon thereafter the same news was brought to the lady Igraine. She stared at the bearer of the tidings. "No," she said. "No, it is not possible."

Her ladies hurried to do what they could for her in her

shock and grief. They could not know the real reason she kept repeating, "No, no, impossible." Nor did Igraine feel able to tell any of them that she had spent the night in the arms of a man she *thought* was her husband. If it had not been he — then who was it?

After the death of Gorlois, his barons came to Uther to ask for peace and accord between him and Igraine. Uther wanted nothing better. The siege was ended. Then Uther sent Ulfius to the barons with his request to marry the widowed Igraine.

It all came about very easily. The barons were glad to be on Uther Pendragon's side instead of against him. The lady Igraine bowed her head and made no objections. Soon the wedding was being celebrated at Tintagel.

Uther Pendragon was so happy that the whole celebration went with a whirl. Few noticed that the lady Igraine was very silent through it all.

Doing everything he could to please Igraine, Uther arranged fine marriages for her two older daughters. Morgawse would be wed to King Lot of the far northern isles of Orkney. Elaine was affianced to King Nentres. Uther also made arrangements for the youngest, Morgan le Fay, to be sent to school at a famous nunnery where it was reputed that the sisters were not only learned in letters but in sorcery.

All these arrangements caused more festivities. But at last all the celebrations were over. And by this time it was clear that the lady Igraine was to bear a child before too long.

"Tell me," said Uther, "who is the child's father. Be honest and I will only love you the more."

Finally Igraine opened her heart and spoke of the mystery that had haunted her ever since the night of Gorlois' death. "Sir," she said, "I will tell you the truth. The same night that my lord met his death, there came to my room a man like my lord in speech and looks and so I welcomed him as a wife would. I thought it was he. I did not know —" She burst into tears.

Uther caught her to him and raised her face. "My love," he said, "it was I who came to you that night, magicked by Merlin to look like your husband."

"You?" she whispered. Then she smiled a little through her tears. "Oh, I am glad. If there had to be magic, I am glad it was you."

She still did not know the price of that magic.

Merlin appeared suddenly one day, looking like himself, with a bushy beard and wild hair, and that was a surprise in itself. "Remember, sire," he said to Uther, "the child is to be delivered to me the night after its birth. I have made all the arrangements."

Igraine was astonished. "Delivered to *you*?"

Uther looked uncomfortable. "I promised," he said to her. "In order to win you."

Igraine gazed at him, taking it in. Then she looked at Merlin. "But why do you want the child, Merlin?"

Merlin stroked his beard slowly. "My lady, you know that I have lived backwards in time," he said. "What is the future to you is the past to me. So I know all about it. It is better for the child, better for England, that you do as I say. However, for your comfort, I will tell you that I have found a worthy knight, Sir Ector, and his wife, to raise the child. You need not fear for its well-being."

With that, he pulled at his beard with both hands and vanished as suddenly as he had appeared.

* * *

The day came when Igraine's child was born, a fine
boy. She held him to her, admiring him. Uther leaned
over the mother and child and he admired the infant
also. But as the hour came close to midnight he was
ordering what had to be done. The baby was wrapped in
cloth of gold, as befitted a king's son. Then he was put in
the arms of one of Igraine's ladies. Another lady and two
knights were appointed to go with her. Then the baby
was carried through the dark, cold, echoing halls of the
castle to the postern gate.

A poorly dressed man was waiting there. The lady
with the child had her instructions. She gave the child
into the old fellow's arms and watched as he and the
child vanished into the night.

So it befell that the infant who would one day become
King Arthur was taken by Merlin to spend the years of
his childhood in the home of Sir Ector and his wife, with
no knowledge at all of his heritage or destiny.

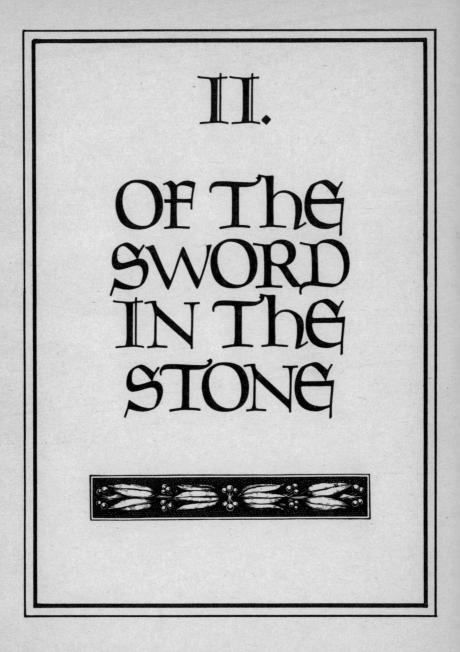

II.

OF THE SWORD IN THE STONE

They galumphed toward each other on old farm horses. Each held in one hand a wooden pole in what they hoped was the proper manner. With the other hand they shielded themselves with a tin tray from the kitchen.

Thud, thud. The heavy hooves of the horses shook the earth as the boys approached each other.

Suddenly, there was a clang as one wooden pole hit a tin tray, and a smaller thud as one boy, unbalanced, fell off his mount while his horse galloped on.

The other boy reined in his mount. "Kay!" he called. "Are you all right?"

The boy on the ground scrambled to his feet. He was frowning. "You came at me the wrong way."

The other answered. "Kay! I came straight as could be. How was it wrong?"

"It was not a fair fall," said the one who was dusting himself off. "Not fair at all."

The one on horseback thought a moment. "Very well.

We will not count it. Do you want to try another?"

"Oh, go away," said the other one, stomping off.

Games between Kay and Arthur often ended this way. Kay, a year older than Arthur, was a bad loser. Arthur, on the other hand, was a good-tempered boy, eager to follow the rules. He took after his mother, Igraine, in his fair-mindedness, though of course he thought Sir Ector's wife was his mother. She had nursed him and cherished him from his earliest days. In the same way, he thought Sir Ector was his father and that Kay was his brother. He roamed the fields and woods around Sir Ector's manor with Kay. He fished the streams with him and he and Kay together learned from Sir Ector the ways of falconing and of jousting.

Some say that during these years of Arthur's boyhood, Merlin came often to the manor, posing as a tutor, to teach the boy—not just the usual letters and numbers—but to encourage him to think about such things as right and wrong, honor and justice, and other abstract matters that might one day worry a king. Perhaps he did. Perhaps he didn't. Merlin was forever popping in and out of people's lives in those days.

Merlin was in and out of Uther Pendragon's life rather often after the King fell ill and the country was invaded by armies from the north.

"Sire," Merlin said, appearing one day looking like one of the poor foot soldiers who did the scrubby, dirty work of fighting, "why do you not come to the battlefield? Your presence there would make us much more able to fight."

"Who are you?" growled Uther. "How did you get in here?" Then he recognized Merlin. "I'm ill," said Uther.

14

"Yes," said Merlin, "I know. But you could be carried on a litter and just knowing you were there would make a difference to the army."

Uther groaned. But he had benefited too much from Merlin's advice to ignore it now. He called his men and had himself dressed and a litter prepared. When at last he appeared at the battlefield, it was as Merlin had predicted. His fighting men were inspired to new efforts and his knights sent the enemy flying.

There was great rejoicing when Uther returned to London after this victory and for a while Uther himself appeared to be recovered. Then he fell ill again and this time no one, not even Merlin with all his magic, could cure him.

And so it befell that Uther Pendragon died and was buried with much ceremony. His wife, Igraine, grieved greatly, and so did the knights who had been close to him.

But in the kingdom at large there came to be much trouble and confusion. It seemed that Uther had died without an heir and no one was sure who should be king of England.

All the great dukes and lords began inventing some claim to the crown, and as they tried to convince others of these claims, dozens of quarrels and even small wars broke out.

Merlin was the only one who knew the truth. But he also knew it would hardly satisfy the nobles of the land just to tell them that a youth named Arthur, living in the country, was Uther's son and his true heir.

Merlin went to the archbishop of Canterbury.

"My lord," he said. "What we need now is some sign

from heaven. If you will summon the barons and dukes and lords of the kingdom to come to London at Christmastime, I do believe God will provide us with some such sign to settle this question."

The archbishop did as Merlin suggested. He sent out a call for all the lords of the land to come to London to celebrate Christmas. As a result a huge crowd was assembled in the great church to hear the services.

After the mass they all streamed out into the frosty air, and lo, before them they saw a strange and marvelous sight. In the center of the churchyard was a great stone of marble on which rested an anvil of steel, and thrust into the anvil was a sword.

They came closer and saw that the hilt of the sword was engraved with letters of gold. And the letters read:

Whoso pulleth out this sword of this stone and anvil is rightwise king born of all England.

Here indeed was the sign from heaven that Merlin had hoped for.

Now the barons, the lords, the dukes, and the knights began pushing and shoving for their chance to grab at the sword hilt and draw the sword from the anvil. Elbowing each other out of the way, they reached for the hilt. And one after another they tugged and pulled at the sword. But it would not budge.

Finally the tumult was so great that the archbishop came out and called an end to the contest.

"He whom God intends must not be here," he said. "Let you all go now and arrange a tourney for New Year's Day when even those who are not here now may appear. After that we will have another trial at the sword in the stone."

Gradually the crowd around the stone broke up and

all went their ways, and the archbishop set up a guard of eight knights to watch over the sword.

Strange as it may seem, Sir Ector, who did not live far from London, had not heeded the archbishop's call to the Christmas mass. From a neighboring squire he heard something about a miraculous sword in a stone but it seemed to have nothing to do with him. He was a man without pretensions. But when he heard of the New Year's tourney he decided this would be a grand outing for himself and the two boys, Kay and Arthur.

The boys were beside themselves with excitement and spent hours in jousting practice, and more hours polishing their swords and breastplates.

Finally they were cantering along beside Sir Ector on their way to London.

And now Merlin was at work again. How else can it be explained that Kay, so anxious to take part in his very first tournament, could have had such a strange lapse of memory? It had to be Merlin, working his magic.

Suddenly Kay was reining in his horse. "My sword," he said. Sir Ector and Arthur reined their horses as well. "What about it?" said Sir Ector.

"I don't have it. I left it at home."

"Left it?" said Sir Ector, astonished.

"I was busy polishing my breastplate," said Kay nervously. "I was grooming my horse…"

"But this is terrible," said Sir Ector. "We are late already for getting good places in the lists."

"I know, I know," said Kay. Then he turned to Arthur. "Arthur, would you please…? I know it's a lot to ask but still—"

Arthur was a good-tempered youth but he was no

17

saint. He was as anxious to go to the tournament as Kay and so he stared ahead with a stubborn look on his face.

"Please, Arthur," said Kay. "I will save you a good place, I promise."

"Oh, all right," said Arthur. He wheeled his horse and galloped back down the road to the manor.

Nobody at home at the manor? All the gates and doors locked? How could this be? Merlin again?

At any rate, Arthur was now both frustrated and angry. "I will get a sword for my brother," he said to himself. He remembered the churchyard they had passed on their way toward London, and that there had been a sword standing in an anvil there. "I will get that one," he thought. And he rode at a gallop toward the church.

The knights who had been set to guard the sword were all off to the tournament. There was no one to stop Arthur as he ran into the churchyard, grasped the hilt of the sword, drew it from the anvil, then ran back to his horse, mounted again, and rode swiftly on to meet his father and brother at the tournament.

He found them at the edge of the crowd. He jumped off his horse and handed the sword to Kay.

"Here," he said. "It is not yours, but it should serve."

"Well, thank you very much," said Kay. Then he looked at the hilt of the sword and he saw the letters in gold to which Arthur had paid no attention.

Whoso pulleth out this sword...is rightwise king born of all England.

Kay gasped and his hand tightened on the sword hilt. He stood a moment and then hurried over to Sir Ector.

18

"Look, father," he said. "See my new sword!"

Sir Ector looked. He saw the golden letters. *Whoso pulleth out this sword...*

He looked at Kay. He spoke slowly. "How—how in heaven's name—did you get this sword?"

Kay would have liked to say that he had pulled it from the anvil himself. But for all his faults, Kay was no liar. Besides, he had been under his father's eyes the whole time since he discovered he was missing his sword.

He took a breath and finally he said, "Arthur brought it to me."

Sir Ector looked over to where Arthur was tying his horse to a tree. Then he went over to him. "Arthur," he said, "how did you get this sword?"

"Sir," said the youth, "there was no one at the manor when I returned there. All the gates were locked. So I went to the churchyard and took the sword from the stone there."

"You pulled it out of the stone?"

"Yes, father. Was it wrong of me to take it? No one was about to say me nay and I thought we could put it back after the tourney."

"You pulled it out of the stone—all by yourself?" Sir Ector repeated.

"Well, yes," said Arthur in a puzzled tone. "How should I need any help in pulling a sword out of an anvil?"

Suddenly Sir Ector was dropping to one knee before Arthur and motioning Kay to kneel also.

Arthur was astonished. "Father, what are you doing? Why are you down on your knees?"

Sir Ector said, "I knew from the time that Merlin brought you to me as an infant that you were of no common birth. But I had not really expected this. Sir, will you be my good and gracious lord when you are king, and will you be kind also to Kay?"

Well, it all took some time, of course. Hard as it was for Arthur to realize that Sir Ector was not his father and Kay not his brother—that he really must be the son of Uther Pendragon and Igraine — it was much, much harder for all the lords, dukes, knights, and barons of England to believe that this youth, come out of nowhere, could really be "rightwise king born of all England."

Contest after contest was held in the churchyard with the sword thrust back into the anvil. One lord, duke, baron, or knight after another tried his best to remove it. Hundreds tried and failed. Then after the trials Arthur once again showed how easily he could take out the sword. Until at last most men were convinced this young man must indeed be the one destined by heaven to be king.

Finally there came the day when Arthur was to be crowned in the great church. All the knights knelt as he passed before them and they asked his pardon for doubting him so long. And Arthur was happy to forgive them all.

When he came to the nave of the church, Arthur lifted the sword which he had removed from the stone and placed it on the high altar, dedicating it to God. After that, the archbishop crowned him king of England.

III.
OF MERLIN'S HELP AND HIS FORGET- FULNESS

Merlin was a wonderful help to the young new king—when he was around. The trouble was, he came and went on some unpredictable schedule of his own.

It would have been easy for Arthur to panic when kings to the west, beyond the Welsh marches, or borders, banded together to try to oust him as a young upstart from his throne. Fortunately, Merlin was on hand then, encouraging the young man and advising him. "Send for King Ban and King Bors from France to come and help you," he said. "They were allies of your father. And of course you will promise your aid to them when it is needed." Arthur did whatever Merlin suggested. He sent for Ban and Bors and they came with a host of fighting men, and with their strength and experience to aid him, Arthur finally was able to push back the western kings into their own little kingdoms.

Most of these battles took place near Carleon where Arthur had a fair-sized castle.

Arthur had found it a little overwhelming at first to have so many castles. There was one in London, of course. And there was one at Camelot, which some people called Winchester. And the one at Carleon, on the Welsh marches. And there were others here and there. But it is easier to grow used to too much than too little and before long Arthur was simply choosing which castle pleased him best.

He was on his way from the castle at Carleon to the one in London when he encountered a knight in the forest who challenged him to a joust. As it happened, this knight was so skilled that Arthur lost his sword and might have lost his life except that Merlin was nearby and put a spell on the rampant knight so that he fell asleep. After that, Merlin found a hermit to tend to Arthur's wounds, and before long they were again on their way.

"But now I have no sword," said Arthur.

Merlin looked rather smug, almost as though he had been waiting for this.

"No matter," he said. "Nearby there is a sword that may be yours if you so wish."

He rode ahead through the trees until the trees parted and they saw before them a broad lake. As they came to the edge of the lake they saw a strange sight. An arm draped in silk arose from the water in the center of the lake, and in its hand it held a sword.

Arthur stared. Appearing out of nowhere, a maiden was gliding over the waters of the lake toward the shore.

"Who is that damsel?" asked Arthur.

"She is the Lady of the Lake," said Merlin, "and if you speak fair to her she will give you that sword."

The maiden approached King Arthur and made a small curtsy before him.

"Damsel," said Arthur, "what sword is that held upward by the arm above the water? I would it were mine for I have no sword."

"Sir King," the maiden replied, "the sword is mine and if you will promise me a gift when I ask it of you, you shall have it."

"By my honor," said Arthur, "I surely promise you a gift if I may have that sword. Just tell me what you wish."

"Yonder is a barge," said the maiden. "Row yourself out to the sword and take it and the scabbard with it. I will ask for my gift at some future time when I am most in need of it."

After that, Arthur and Merlin both dismounted and tied their horses to a tree. They went to the barge and Arthur poled them out across the lake to the mysterious upthrust arm holding the sword. When they came to it, Arthur reached out and took the sword in its scabbard and the arm disappeared into the lake. And when they turned to pole themselves back to shore the maiden who was known as the Lady of the Lake had also disappeared.

And that was how it befell that Arthur acquired his famous sword, Excalibur, which had a magic of its own, and the scabbard also, which would sometimes glow with a dazzling brightness when Arthur was riding against a challenger. As for the gift that Arthur promised the Lady of the Lake, that was not asked of him for some years and is part of another story.

But of course it was Merlin who led him to the lake, Merlin who saved him from the rampaging knight in the forest, Merlin who had guided him through those frightening battles with the western kings.

But where was Merlin a few months later when he should have been warning Arthur against the great mistake of his life? He was off somewhere, busy about his own affairs. And Arthur was at Carleon again, a castle he liked quite well, when a beautiful visitor arrived.

Her name was Morgawse. She was the wife of King Lot of the Orkney Isles and she had four sons: Gawaine, Gaheris, Agravaine,and Gareth, two of whom (the two oldest) she brought with her. She was not only beautiful, in a dark and brooding way, but also she was skilled at witchcraft.

It is hard to know why she wanted young Arthur as a conquest. Perhaps just to make mischief. But whatever the reason, it was all easy enough for Morgawse to put a spell on him, and Arthur was totally bewitched by her while she stayed at Carleon.

She left with her sons, and the spell she had put upon him lifted. He shook his head to clear it of the cobwebs of magic and stared about in a sort of wonder. What had happened? How could he have been so bemused by that woman? Beautiful, yes—but older than he by fifteen or twenty years. And her mouth, now that he recalled it, had a small, cruel edge to its smile.

Then, finally, Merlin came back from his excursions and heard who had been with Arthur at Carleon.

"Morgawse!" he said and grabbed at his beard. "But surely I told you...!"

"Told me what?" asked Arthur.

Now Merlin grabbed at his hair. "How could I have forgotten? I meant to warn you—meant to tell you—"

26

"Merlin," said Arthur. "Tell me plainly what you mean." He had never before spoken so sharply to Merlin but something about the magician's behavior was frightening him. "Tell me," he said again.

"May day, May day," cried the magician, tearing at his hair. "On May day will be born the one who spells your doom."

"I do not understand," said Arthur.

"Through my fault," said Merlin, "because I forgot to warn you. So now you must do as I tell you. You must send out an edict that all boy children of the kingdom born on this next May day must be...must be — " Merlin hesitated, as if he was not sure exactly what must be done. Then he went on. "They must all be put on a ship and sent out to sea."

"Babies?" said Arthur, horrified. "Sent out to sea?"

"Have I ever told you wrong before?"

"But that would be terrible. What would happen to them? Would they survive? Who would care for them?"

"Will you issue the edict as I tell you or must I bewitch you?" said Merlin.

Actually, Arthur was tired of being bewitched. He had had enough of it with Morgawse. Also, he had always obeyed Merlin.

But—babies put out to sea in a ship?

"I can issue the edict, if you authorize me," said Merlin. Suddenly he was no longer pulling at his beard, but very firm. "Authorize me, sire. It must be done."

And so the order went out across the kingdom. All boy babies born on May day must be delivered to a ship that would put in at one port after another to take on the infants.

The thing was done. The ship put out to sea and went

about collecting its pitiful cargo. Soon thereafter it was wrecked in a storm and many of the children perished. However, there were some who survived. One was washed ashore in a rough cradle. A good knight, walking by chance along the shore, saw the infant in his basket, took him home, and reared him tenderly.

This was the child named Mordred, son of Morgawse, born to her after her bewitchment of Arthur at Carleon. Later, through her magic, Morgawse would find the boy and keep him with her for a while, and then take him to King Arthur's court.

By then, Arthur would have learned the fact that Merlin forgot to tell him. Morgawse, who had bewitched him, was the oldest daughter of Igraine, and so Arthur's own half-sister.

But all the troubles that would come from that were a long time in the future.

Soon after the terrible May day command, some much happier events took place.

Arthur found himself a queen and established his Round Table.

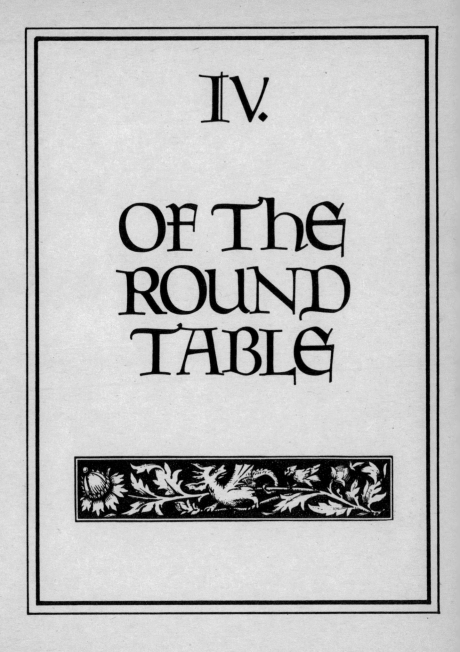

IV.

OF THE ROUND TABLE

This time Merlin was not going to be caught napping or forgetful.

"No, sire," he told Arthur, "she is not the one for you."

"But why?" asked Arthur. "She is the daughter of a king, and a very loyal king, too. She is very young and very beautiful."

"Nevertheless," said Merlin.

"Nevertheless what?" said Arthur.

"There is something. A long shadow."

"A shadow around Guenevere? But she is the most like sunshine of anyone I ever knew. Yes, that is really the word that describes her best—sunshiny. She is all golden and open and loving and kind."

"Sunlight casts a shadow," said Merlin. "There is a long, long shadow behind her."

"See here," said Arthur, "the barons have all been telling me for a long time that I should get married. You have said so too."

31

Merlin nodded.

"Then you ask if there is anyone I favor and I tell you, yes. Guenevere, daughter of King Leodegrance. From the first moment I saw her I knew that she was the one I could love all my life."

"But sire"—and now Merlin spoke desperately—"she will not be true."

"Guenevere not be true? Oh, I cannot believe that, Merlin. You can tell just by looking at her that trueness is what you can count on."

Merlin shook his head, pulled at his beard, and said, "Yes, yes, that is so. But there is this shadow."

"You are not making much sense," said Arthur.

"She is true — and untrue," said Merlin.

"Oh, that is ridiculous. I love Guenevere," Arthur said. "And I wish you would go at once to King Leodegrance and ask if I may have her hand in marriage."

At this Merlin lifted his shoulders in a shrug and sighed. This time he had tried to alter events and to prevent what he feared was going to happen from happening. And he had not succeeded. Events would go as they were fated.

He magicked himself off to the court of King Leodegrance and arrayed now in his best wizard's robe and most impressive hat he presented Arthur's request.

Leodegrance was delighted with everything. With Merlin in his mystic outfit, with the news that King Arthur wanted to marry his daughter.

"Nothing would please me better," he said. "And when they wed, my gift to Arthur will be that great Table Round which his father, Uther, once gave to me. And with it I will send one hundred of my best knights."

Arthur had now taken up residence at his castle in Camelot, the one he was beginning to think he liked best of all. And so Merlin traveled to Camelot along with a great train of people. Guenevere, dressed in rich silks and velvets, with filmy veils that flew up about her head and sometimes across her eyes, rode in a fine litter with her ladies-in-waiting around her. A huge wagon conveyed the Table Round, and King Leodegrance himself cantered cheerfully in the lead of his hundred knights.

Arthur, usually so calm, was in a fine state of jitters as he waited for their arrival. He had long since appointed his foster brother, Sir Kay, to be his chief steward, in charge of all the furnishing and provisioning of the various castles. Now he dragged Sir Kay around with him, suggesting all sorts of improvements—new tapestries in the great hall ("Much too late for anything like that, Arthur," said Kay), a fine new bed for what would be the bridal chamber ("Well, yes. I don't see why not."), and an absolutely endless supply of fine food and drink for the company ("But of course, sire," said Kay, looking offended. "Haven't you always been able to depend on me for that?").

Finally the great company arrived at Camelot and Arthur went to kneel before Guenevere. "Fair lady," he said, "you are more than passing welcome for I have loved you long."

Guenevere stepped down from her litter. She took his hand and raised him up and looked at him with her open, sunny smile and said, "My lord, I am happy to be here."

*   *   *

After that, the great Round Table was unloaded from its wagon and set up in the main hall of the castle at Camelot. Around it were placed one hundred and fifty seats — or sieges, the courtly word for seats. On each siege was inscribed in letters of gold the name of the knight who would sit there. King Leodegrance had already brought one hundred knights to fill that many seats which did not leave too many for Arthur's men. But Sir Kay was quickly assigned a seat, and so was Sir Ector, his foster father, and Sir Ulfius, who had been a friend to Uther Pendragon. Other loyal knights were given their places and because the table was round, all were equal as they sat about it.

But Merlin stopped Arthur at one seat and shook his head. The golden letters read, "Siege Perilous."

"What does that mean?" asked Arthur.

"It is a seat reserved for the perfect knight," said Merlin. "Anyone else sits in it on peril of instant death."

"Well," said Arthur. "A perfect knight. What would he be like, and do you suppose one such will come to Camelot?"

Merlin gave one of his shrugs. "You will know it plainly when he does," he said.

Then, as it happened, while seats were still being assigned, a young man came to Arthur, asking to be knighted. He was a fair, strong fellow who had traveled all the way from the far isles of Orkney to Arthur's court. Arthur asked his name.

"Gawaine," he said, "son of King Lot of Orkney and of Morgawse."

A small shudder ran up Arthur's spine as he heard that name and remembered a dark beauty and other dark things. But the young man before him had nothing to do with any of that. He looked to be a proper knight and Arthur knew him as his nephew.

"Indeed I will knight you, with a right good will," said Arthur. He tapped Gawaine lightly on his shoulder with his sword. And magically, Gawaine's name appeared in gold on one of the sieges around the great Table.

With all of this, preparations had been going forward for the wedding of Arthur and Guenevere. Finally, all was ready.

The two stood before the archbishop in the church of Saint Stephen and made their vows. And then with choirs singing, all manner of sweet instruments playing, and everyone bowing as they walked back up the aisle, they left the church and were carried to the castle where a great feast had been prepared.

The knights were all gathered around the great Table Round when Arthur and Guenevere appeared to take their places. The knights stood, doing homage to their king and their new queen, lifting goblets high and wishing them long life and endless happiness.

Then the food came in a rushing tide of platters and trenchers—roasted boar, roasted venison, roasted hare, little birds toasted, big birds stuffed, big pies, little pies, suckling pig. There seemed no end to it. Sir Kay had done his job well. And, of course, great pitchers of ale and wine went round and round the huge table.

Arthur sat beside Guenevere, not eating much, but looking around the table from one face to another, smiling a little, and thinking he had never before been so happy, so satisfied.

But because he was Arthur, the fairminded, and because he was king, he had to remember at this moment that others in his kingdom were not so happy. He had traveled about enough, since he had become king, to see a good deal of violence and cruelty and suffering. It had hurt him to see this and he had wondered why it had to be and what he, now that he was king, could do about it. Suddenly, sitting there amidst all the warmth and light and happiness and with his bride beside him, he thought what a mighty force of strength and courage was ringed around him. And he thought of how that strength might be used to fight against the forces that caused needless suffering.

And then, the good, even-tempered young man, who had never shown many signs of imagination, was struck with the idea that would make him immortal.

He rose to his feet and spoke to the knights around him. "We are happy here today, safe and secure. But out across the kingdom there are many who are not happy. Many who live in fear. Robbers and murderers lurk in the woods and the byways, terrifying travelers. There are giants and ogres and bad men who kidnap young maidens, defraud old people, abuse children." He paused a moment, thinking how to phrase what he wanted to say next, and the pause only made everyone look up and wait with more attention.

"Look," he said then. "What I want to say is, you are all of you the bravest and best men in the kingdom. But you spend a good deal of your time challenging and fighting each other. What about spending more time fighting the robbers and murderers, the frauds and cheats?"

A silence had fallen on all those around the table. Arthur went on rather desperately. "Why shouldn't we all band together to fight against whatever is wrong and cruel? Let us have a new fellowship, a fellowship of the Round Table, where each of us vows just that—to fight against the wrong and help the helpless. Will you all vow that with me?"

There was rustling and a stirring all around the table and then a great racket as chairs were pushed back and one knight after another stood to take the vow. "To fight against injustice and to right wrongs and help the helpless."

Arthur had a shining look as he gazed around at the knights. "From now on this will be your questing when you go out looking for adventure. And after this, each year at this time you will return here to Camelot and the Round Table to tell of what you have achieved in this kind of quest." He raised his goblet to all those who were assembled and took a sip. He sat down and looked with love on Guenevere.

And in this way was born the order of the Knights of the Round Table whose deeds would become so famous.

V.

OF SIR LAUNCELOT

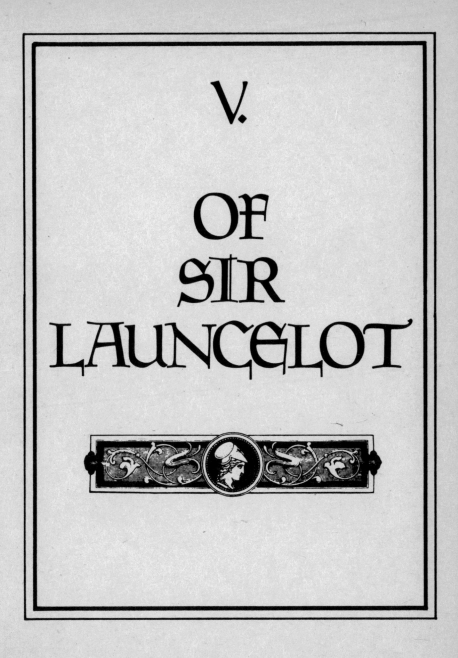

The idea of the Round Table caught on among ambitious young men everywhere. They came flocking to Camelot from the east and the west to be King Arthur's knights. Two more of Morgawse's sons came from the Orkneys, Gaheris and Agravaine. And young men came from Ireland and from France.

Among those who came from France was one who was destined to become the most famous of all King Arthur's knights. His full name was Galahad Launcelot du Lac, and he was a son of King Ban of Benwick, who had helped Arthur in his earliest battles. Somehow, word of the Round Table idea had come to the young Launcelot and after that he could think of nothing but how he might become a member of that fellowship. Through the years of his boyhood he practiced at tilting and jousting and fencing and every one of the knightly skills until he was adept at them all.

At last he was able to realize his dream and make his way to King Arthur's court.

"Rise, Sir Launcelot," said Arthur, and the young man who had knelt to be knighted got to his feet. He and Arthur looked at each other a moment and in the time that they looked each knew they were born to be friends.

"Come," said Arthur. "Let me take you to meet Guenevere." He clapped his hand on Launcelot's shoulder and led the way down the long corridor, hung with tapestries, to the sunny rooms at the back of the castle, where Guenevere and her ladies liked to sit at their sewing and weaving.

"Gwen, my dear," Arthur called, "come and meet the newest addition to the Round Table, Sir Launcelot du Lac."

Guenevere got up from the window seat and a shaft of sunlight from the window cast a glow around her as she came toward them. She dipped a small curtsy and then rose saying, "Sir Launcelot, you are most welcome."

As Guenevere looked full into Launcelot's eyes and he looked into hers, their gazes locked and a strange shock went through them both.

Years later, Launcelot would call himself Le Chevalier Mal Fait, which could mean different things, among the meanings being that he was an Ill-Made Knight, not handsome and even-featured as some men were.

Perhaps he did have a rough, craggy face. If so, it made no difference to Guenevere. Just as Arthur and Launcelot had looked at each other and recognized that they were friends, now Guenevere and Launcelot recognized something else—an electric connection between them that seemed to keep their eyes and hands fused together.

It only seemed to the two of them that it was a long

time before she broke away. And for all the sunshine in the room, the light threw no shadow behind Guenevere as she went to pick up her sewing again. The shadow around that sunshiny lady which Merlin had foreseen had not yet darkened.

They loved each other purely and happily.

Launcelot was content to ride in the jousts and tourneys which Arthur was holding, day after day. It was happiness for him to ride at his opponent, his spear fewtered, and then to unhorse him in one charge. After the jousting he stood before Arthur and Arthur praised his skill, saying, "You win your worthship over and over again, Lance." And all the while Guenevere would be smiling her admiration. The electricity tingled between him and her but they enjoyed it innocently.

The time came for Launcelot to go off on his year of questing. His two brothers, Sir Lionel and Sir Ector de Maris, had now come from France to join the Round Table and Sir Lionel chose to ride forth with his brother, Sir Launcelot.

They took leave of Arthur, and Launcelot kissed Guenevere's hand and looked into her eyes for another of those shaking moments. Then they clambered onto their horses. No knight, clothed in heavy armor, was able to leap onto a horse. And off they went.

They rode and rode, through the hours of the morning. Adventure was not around every turn of the road then any more than it is today. They were still riding at noon with the sun hot and high in the sky. Launcelot became so drowsy that he reined his horse and said, "Brother, let us stop and rest a while."

They dismounted and tied their horses to an apple tree and lay down on the ground.

Launcelot was soon deep asleep. But Sir Lionel lay awake. Presently he heard the pounding of hooves and then he saw three knights riding as hard as they could while another knight, who seemed huge in his armor, pursued them.

As Lionel watched, the huge knight overtook first one, then the second, then the third knight, and one after the other, he smote them down with his sword. As each fell from his horse, he bound that knight with the reins of his own mount and slung him across the horse's back.

Sir Lionel jumped to his feet, ran to untie his horse, and was soon thumping after the huge knight and his captives.

"Turn," Sir Lionel called. "Turn and face me."

The huge knight did turn and raced at Sir Lionel and in two seconds he struck Sir Lionel to the ground. After that he bound him as the other knights were bound, threw him across his horse and went on again, now with four captive knights, toward his castle. There he threw all his captives into a dungeon which was already crowded with knights who had met the same fate.

By chance, Sir Ector de Maris, Sir Launcelot's other brother, who had also ridden out that morning, encountered the huge knight as he was coming out of his castle. Before long, Sir Ector had been vanquished also and was being tossed into the dungeon.

He saw his brother, Sir Lionel. "Alas, Lionel," he cried, "you too?"

And Lionel could only say the same thing back.

44

"Who is this monster knight who overcomes us so easily?" asked Ector.

Lionel had learned his name from the other knights in the dungeon. "He is Sir Turquine, and I greatly fear that unless Launcelot comes to our rescue we may never be delivered. I have never seen anyone else to match Sir Turquine."

"Nor I," said Ector.

Meanwhile, through all the pounding of hooves and falling of bodies and cries and shouting as Sir Turquine made his conquests, Sir Launcelot had slept on beneath the apple tree.

He was still asleep, as if bewitched, when four queens came riding down the forest way. They were escorted by four knights who, with four staffs, held a great canopy of green silk over the ladies so that they should not suffer from the sun.

They came near the tree and saw the knight asleep and they reined their horses. And one among them, who was Morgan le Fay, half-sister of King Arthur, recognized Sir Launcelot du Lac, finest of Arthur's knights.

"Ah," said one of the queens, "I would like to have such a knight for my love."

"I too," said the second.

"I fancy him greatly" said the third.

Morgan Le Fay looked around at them sharply. Then she said, "If anyone should have first choice, it is I. However, we will not argue. I will put an enchantment on him and take him to my castle. Later, we will all go to him and let him choose which of us he will have."

And so it was done.

A few hours later Launcelot awoke from his sleep in a

strange, cold chamber that he had never seen before and he wondered greatly what had happened.

Then the four queens came to him and all of them were fair to see and covered with rich silks and fine jewels.

"Now you must choose which of us you will love," said Morgan le Fay. "Either that or stay in this prison and die."

"Well," said Launcelot, "this is a hard case. I have no wish to die. Yet would I rather die here than have any one of you as a love."

"What?" shrieked Morgan le Fay. (She was the youngest of Igraine's daughters, you may remember, and had been spoiled somewhat at the nunnery, along with being taught magic.) "You refuse all of us?" she yelled.

"I do," said Launcelot. "You are all enchantresses and witches."

"Indeed," cried one. "How dare you?" cried another. "Listen to him!" said the third.

"Very well," said Morgan le Fay now, in a steely voice. "You can stay here and rot."

"Yes," said the others. "Rot." Then they all left and locked him into the cold, dark chamber.

After a long time, a damsel came with some food for him. "What cheer, Sir Knight?" she asked.

"Truly, fair damsel," said Launcelot, "in all my life, never so ill."

"I am sorry," she said. "Very sorry. But they tell me you are Sir Launcelot du Lac, the finest knight in the world, and my father has great need of a good knight to fight for him in a tournament next week. If you could agree to help him perhaps I could help you."

"Who is your father?" asked Launcelot.

"King Bagdemagus, sir. And he had very ill fortune in his last tournament. If things do not go better for him this next time I do not know what will happen."

"Bagdemagus," said Launcelot. "I know he is a good knight and I will gladly help him if I can escape this enchanted prison."

And so it came about that the next day the damsel came with food for Sir Launcelot, but this time she took him out past twelve locked doors and brought him to the place where his armor had been stored, and then to his horse.

After that, Launcelot rode with her to the castle of her father, King Bagdemagus, and offered the king his services in the tournament.

Launcelot wore no emblems or signs on his arms to make known who he was when he rode into the lists. But it was not long before everyone knew that some unusual knight was fighting for King Bagdemagus. When the tourney was over, Launcelot had struck down all sixteen knights who had ridden out against him.

There was great good cheer in the castle afterward as King Bagdemagus thanked Launcelot for his help. But now Launcelot was eager to ride out and discover what had happened to his brother, Sir Lionel, while he himself had been asleep.

So Launcelot rode forth and by good fortune made his way to the same forest where he had fallen asleep. In those woods he met a maiden who told him of Sir Turquine's castle nearby where the huge knight kept many of King Arthur's knights as prisoners.

Just then Sir Turquine himself came riding by with still another knight bound across his horse. Launcelot recognized this poor captured fellow as Gaheris, Gawaine's brother.

"Ho!" cried Launcelot. "Release that knight or I will see to it that you do!"

But of course Sir Turquine was not about to do any releasing just because someone called at him to do so.

In no time, Launcelot and Turquine were fewtering their spears and galloping toward each other. Soon both were unhorsed and fighting on foot. Finally both paused to get their breaths.

When Sir Turquine could speak at last without panting, he said, "Surely you are the best knight I ever fought, but somehow you remind me of one knight that I hate above all others. If you are not he, I will give you that captive yonder—I will free all the knights in my dungeon as well, and you and I can be friends all our lives long."

"A generous offer," said Launcelot. "Now tell me what knight you hate above all others."

"Truly," answered Sir Turquine, "it is Sir Launcelot du Lac. He slew my brother and it is because of him that I have captured so many knights from King Arthur's court. Tell me you are not he and we can be friends."

"That I cannot tell you," said Launcelot, "for indeed, I am Sir Launcelot du Lac, King Ban of Benwick's son, knight of the Round Table." He picked up his sword again. "Now I defy you to do your best."

"Ah," said Sir Turquine, picking up his sword, "we shall not part till one or the other is dead."

At that they ran against each other again, thrusting and feinting and thrusting again, until both men were wounded and both very tired. And then, with a quick, clever thrust, Launcelot had triumphed and Sir Turquine was fallen dead.

Launcelot rode now to Sir Turquine's castle, and there he found not only his brother, Sir Lionel, but Sir Ector de Maris, and all the other knights who had been imprisoned. There was much rejoicing as the prisoners came out into the sunlight. Finally they all went off on their separate ways.

This adventure was not the end of Launcelot's year of questing. He rode south into Cornwall, and there he fought with two giants who were keeping many damsels prisoner in a castle, forcing them to work day and night at making tapestries. He killed the giants and the damsels knelt before him in their gratitude.

Launcelot asked the name of the castle where they had been imprisoned and they told him it was called Tintagel.

This was the castle that had once been the home of the lady Igraine. It was the birthplace of Arthur and by good chance Launcelot knew this and could reclaim that castle by the sea for King Arthur.

He rode on and met with more adventures, fighting with this knight and that, and when he overthrew each one he told the knight to travel to Camelot and yield himself to Queen Guenevere.

One time it came about that he was able to rescue Sir Kay, King Arthur's foster brother, from three knights who were pursuing him. These knights, too, he sent to Camelot to surrender to Guenevere.

Another time he had to fight off a love enchantment as he had fought off Morgan le Fay and the three queens.

But his love for Guenevere kept him strong against such potions and bewitchments.

Finally, a year had passed and Launcelot rode back to Camelot. King Arthur greeted him with joy.

"We will all gather around the Round Table and you will tell us your adventures," he said.

Meantime, Guenevere was smiling and nodding and Launcelot felt her gaze on him like the sun.

Later, when everyone had gathered at the Round Table, some of the knights whom Launcelot had overthrown came to surrender themselves to the queen. Guenevere blushed and smiled and put her hands to her cheeks. She had never received such a tribute before.

Then each told some story of how Launcelot had done this or done that and no one doubted that this knight, whether he called himself "Mal Fait" or not, was the finest knight in the world.

And the shadow which Merlin predicted had not yet fallen.

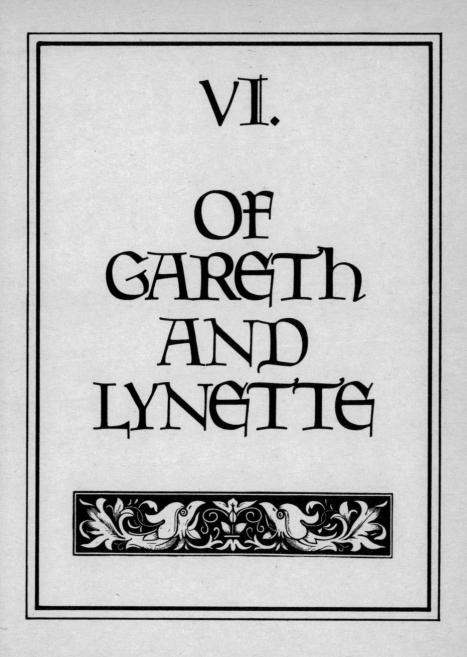

VI.

OF GARETH AND LYNETTE

Off in the far Orkney Isles, where winters were dark and long and even summer wore a chilly smile, Gareth was the only son left at home with Morgawse. But now he was of an age when all he wanted was to join his brothers, Gawaine, Agravaine, and Gaheris, at King Arthur's court.

"No," said Morgawse. "I want you here."

"But Mother," said Gareth, "what is there for me to do on this desolate isle?"

"Do? You can fish. You can hunt. You can follow the deer."

"Follow the deer!" said Gareth. "I would rather follow the king. Live pure, speak true, right wrong, follow the king—else wherefore born!"

"What a lot of fancy talk," said his mother. "You can live pure and speak true right here in Orkney. And I suppose there are wrongs to right here also."

"Mother," said Gareth desperately, "you must let me go."

Morgawse tapped a fingernail against her teeth. It annoyed her very much that Arthur had won her other sons away from her and that now this one wanted to go also.

"All right," she said finally. "You can go on certain conditions."

"Tell me," said Gareth eagerly.

"When you go to King Arthur's court you will not tell him who you are, and you will stay clear of your brothers, and not make yourself known to them either. You will ask to work in the kitchens."

"In the kitchens?"

"Yes," said his mother. "You will work in the kitchens for a year before you ask Arthur to knight you."

Gareth thought it over. Then he said, "One can be free in one's heart however one serves. I will be able to see the jousts and tourneys. And to go unnamed for a year— perhaps that would not be so bad."

So it befell that young Gareth traveled south to Arthur's court in Camelot and went before the king and made his homage. And Arthur asked him what he wished.

"Three wishes," said Gareth, "but only one just now. The other two I would ask of you a year from now."

"What is the one now?" asked Arthur.

"I would like to work in your kitchens."

"What?" said Arthur. The young man before him did not look at all like anyone used to working over spits and kettles.

"Yes," said Gareth, "and then at the end of the year I will make my other requests."

"Who are you?" said Arthur. "What is your name and where do you come from with such strange wishes?"

Gareth shook his head. "I am just someone who wants to work in your kitchens for a year, sire — and then speak to you again of two other wishes."

Arthur studied the large, fair young man, but odd as his request was, he could see no reason not to grant it.

So Gareth went to work in the kitchens of Camelot. And here the one who supervised everything was Sir Kay.

Sir Kay took one look at the big, good-looking young man and to him, also, it seemed strange that such a youth would want to work in the kitchens. He decided that the young man had been raised someplace where food was scarce and that he was greedy for the meats and sauces and soups he could lap up in the kitchen. He noticed also that the young man's hands were large and white, and since the youth gave him no other name, he called him Beaumains, or Pretty Hands.

And now, through the next months, whenever Sir Kay went through the kitchens and spied the man he called Beaumains he cried out some teasing remark. "Are you getting enough grease, Beaumains?" or, "Did you have your share of the roasted pig today?"

Now and then, Sir Launcelot chanced to walk through the kitchens and once he overheard Sir Kay teasing the young man. He went over and started a conversation with him and realized here was an educated and intelligent person. He asked no questions but after that he went out of his way to speak to Gareth, or Beaumains, as he was known, whenever he saw him.

And so the year passed.

And then one day there came a damsel to the castle who made her way to King Arthur.

"I come from a lady of great reknown," she said, "who

is in the power of a terrible tyrant. He keeps her prisoner in her own castle and destroys her lands. I pray for one of your knights to come and rescue her."

"Fair damsel," said Arthur, "tell me your name and your lady's and where she lives."

"My name is Lynette," said the damsel. "The lady for whom I speak is my sister, Dame Lyonesse, and the tyrant who besieges her is called the Red Knight of the Red Lawns."

"I have never heard of him," said Arthur.

"Wait a bit," said Sir Gawaine, who was standing nearby. "I have. In fact, I met with him once and barely escaped with my life. He is as strong as seven men."

"That is true," said the damsel. "He is very powerful. So I beg you, sire, will you send a knight to my sister's rescue?"

Just then the kitchen boy called Beaumains stepped forward. "Sire," he said, "you may remember that a year ago I asked you for three wishes."

Arthur looked at the young man and he did remember. He nodded.

"Sire," Beaumains said, "I have now served in your kitchens for a year as I asked to do. Now I would claim the other two boons. First—that I be given this adventure of the damsel."

"What?" cried the damsel, outraged.

But Arthur looked at the young man. He saw by his bearing and heard by his speech that he was fit and able for better things than kitchen work.

"Very well," he said.

"No!" cried the damsel. "Never!"

"Second," Beaumains went on, "I would be knighted by Sir Launcelot and no other."

Arthur looked over at Sir Launcelot, who studied Beaumains for a moment and then nodded.

Arthur said, "It shall be done."

"No, no, fie!" cried the damsel Lynette. "I want a knight, not a kitchen boy." And she ran out of the hall and mounted her horse and galloped away.

Of course the knighting could not be done in a moment. Launcelot wanted to test the young man at jousting. But after he and Beaumains had ridden at each other a time or two, Launcelot knew that Beaumains had the needed knightly skills. Then he begged to know the young man's true name. Beaumains was silent a moment and then he asked if Launcelot would keep it secret. Launcelot promised and then Beaumains told him that he was really Gareth, son of Lot and Morgawse, and brother of Gawaine and Gaheris and Agravaine.

"I knew it must be something like that," said Launcelot, and he touched the young man on the shoulder with his sword and dubbed him Sir Beaumains for the time being, Sir Gareth when he was ready to assume his real name again.

Then Sir Beaumains galloped off to find the damsel whose adventure he was undertaking.

At last he saw her ahead in the forest, and rode quickly up to her.

When she saw who it was she cried, "You! What are you doing here? You stink of the kitchen. Go away, you washer of dishes."

"Damsel," said Sir Beaumains, "I cannot go away from you. I am the one chosen by King Arthur to rescue your sister and I shall do so or die in the trying."

"How can you rescue anyone," she sneered. "You, stirrer of soups!"

She kicked at her horse to hurry it along and rode on pretending she was alone. But Sir Beaumains followed steadily beside her.

They rode until they came out of the woods into a field that was strangely black. At the edge of the field was a black tree and on it there hung a black banner and a black shield. Beside the tree stood a great black horse and beside the horse was a knight all armed in black.

"Ha," said Lynette. "There is the Knight of the Black Lawns and you had better hurry back into the woods."

"I thank you," said Sir Beaumains, "for always taking me for a coward."

As they spoke, the Black Knight came up to the damsel. "Is this the knight from King Arthur's court that you have brought as a champion?" he asked.

"Indeed not," said Lynette. "This is just a miserable kitchen knave who insists on following me."

"In that case," said the Black Knight, "I will see to it that he bothers you no longer." With that he mounted his horse and rode toward Sir Beaumains crying, "Off you go, kitchen knave!"

But Sir Beaumains was ready with his spear fewtered and he rode at the Black Knight and the two came together with a crash. The Black Knight's spear broke as it struck Beaumains' shield and Beaumains' spear pierced the Black Knight's armor, but it also broke. Both drew their swords and thrust at each other back and forth for more than an hour. Both were bleeding and hurting and very weary. Suddenly, Beaumains struck one mighty blow and the Black Knight fell from his horse and was finished.

Beaumains took for himself the Black Knight's horse and his armor and he rode to where Lynette had been waiting for the outcome of the fight.

"Alas," she cried when he came near, "has a kitchen boy like you killed such a fine knight? Go away from me! Go!"

"I have already told you, fair damsel, I will not leave you until I have accomplished the purpose of this adventure, or else die in trying. Therefore lead on—and I will follow."

"Oh, oh," moaned the damsel. But it seemed there was nothing to do but travel on.

So she and Beaumains traveled together until they saw riding toward them a knight dressed all in green, both his horse and his harness. As he came near he called, "Is that my brother, the Black Knight?"

Lynette called back, "No, it is a miserable kitchen knave who has killed your brother and taken his horse and armor."

After that, what else could happen but that the Green Knight should challenge Beaumains? They ran together with their spears fixed and when their spears broke they used their swords and when they were both unhorsed they still thrust at each other. And then, with one sharp stroke on the helm, Beaumains laid the Green Knight flat on his back. As Beaumains stood over him with his sword at his neck the Green Knight pled for mercy.

"It all depends on the damsel whom I serve," said Beaumains. "If she asks, I will save your life." Lynette came near saying, "Fie, fie, you kitchen slavey, if you think I will ask for anything."

"Then," said Beaumains, "this fellow dies."

"No, no," cried the Green Knight. "Save me and I will forgive you my brother's death. I will become your man and pledge thirty knights of mine to do your bidding also."

"Sir Knight," said Beaumains, "such promises will not move me. Only if this damsel speaks for you will you live." He let the sharp, bright tip of his sword touch the knight's throat.

"No," cried Lynette. "Let be, let be. Do not kill him."

"Damsel," said Sir Beaumains, "your charge is my pleasure. At your command his life shall be saved."

So Beaumains saved the Green Knight. And that night the Green Knight and thirty of his men served Beaumains and Lynette and watched over them.

The next morning Beaumains bid them go to Camelot and make their allegiance to King Arthur and they all raised their hands to their visors in obedience.

Lynette shook her head. "Shame," she said, "shame when good knights obey a kitchen boy."

"Lady," said Sir Beaumains, "when you see me beaten or disgraced you may say shame. Until then, lead on — and I will follow."

The damsel looked at him and sighed. "Very well," she said, "but soon now we will be meeting someone whom you will not overcome, kitchen boy."

She spurred her horse and rode on. And by and by they came out of the woods onto a rise of land and saw in the distance a fine castle. Before it on a broad plain were many pavilions, all the color of indigo.

"Here is the domain of the Knight of Inde," said Lynette. "He is the strongest knight of any except the Red Knight who holds my sister prisoner. So now I advise you to turn back and save yourself."

"Lady," said Sir Beaumains, "you know such words

are of no avail. I will ride forth now and find this Knight of Inde."

He rode down onto the plain and the Knight of Inde came to meet him. He was a splendid sight, dressed all in indigo with his horse's trappings in the same color also.

The Knight of Inde held up his arm and challenged Beaumains to go any further.

So there it was again. Sir Beaumains was fewtering his spear and he and the Knight of Inde were running against each other.

For two hours and more they fought, first on horseback, and then on foot. They gave each other such terrible blows that blood was flowing from each. Then Beaumains was able to land one of his mighty blows across the Knight of Inde's helmet and the knight fell to the ground. Sir Beaumains unlaced the knight's indigo helmet and stood over him with his sword.

"I yield me," said the Knight of Inde. "Have mercy."

The damsel, Lynette, came running, and she cried out, "Spare him! Spare him!"

And Beaumains said, "Gladly will I do so. It would be a pity for such a good knight to die."

Now as the fallen knight's men came running to see to his wounds, the damsel, Lynette, looked down at her shoes and spoke with a different sort of voice to Beaumains.

"You are not really a kitchen knave at all, are you? You are someone of high and noble birth. Why have you gone about pretending?"

"Lady," answered Beaumains, "have I pretended anything with you—or done anything but try to serve you and accomplish your mission?"

Suddenly Lynette looked up and faced him. "Well, I

am sorry for the way I have talked to you. I have not been nice at all and I wish you would forgive me."

"But of course I forgive you, with all my heart," said Beaumains. "And I am not sorry for anything you said. Perhaps it made me try harder."

And so Lynette made peace with Beaumains at last. That night the Knight of Inde entertained them in his castle. He fed them well. He promised Beaumains to go to Arthur and pledge his allegiance. And over and over, he praised the young man who had overthrown him, even comparing him to Sir Launcelot, the greatest of them all.

Still, he warned Beaumains that the last and greatest peril still lay ahead—his meeting with the Red Knight of the Red Lawns.

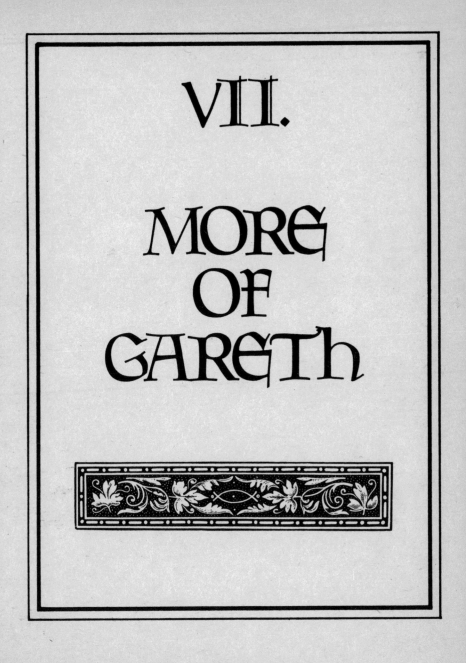

VII.

MORE OF GARETH

A dwarf from the castle of the Knight of Inde took the news to the lady Lyonesse in the Castle Perilous where the Red Knight was holding her prisoner.

"Your sister is on the way," the dwarf said, "bringing with her a knight from King Arthur's court who will rescue you."

"Sir Launcelot?" cried the lady eagerly.

"No, it is not Launcelot," said the dwarf.

The lady's smile faded. "Then what use?" she said. "Who but the finest knight in the world can overcome the Red Knight?"

"Perhaps this one," said the dwarf, and then he proceeded to tell her of some of Beaumains' achievements.

He had been instructed in this story by the Knight of Inde himself. The night before, when the knight was entertaining Lynette and Beaumains, he had begged to know more about the young man. Lynette, atoning for her bad behavior to Beaumains in the past, had told the

65

Inde Knight about his victories over the Black Knight and the Green Knight and the other ways he had shown his courage. Finally, the Inde Knight had begged to know Beaumains' true name and after swearing both Lynette and the knight to secrecy, Beaumain had told them. He was, in fact, Gareth, son of Lot and Morgawse of Orkney.

"Ah," said the Inde Knight. "Now I do not wonder so much at your triumph over me."

The dwarf too had been warned not to tell anyone about Beaumains' true name. He was simply to reassure the lady Lyonesse that rescue was on the way.

The lady thanked the dwarf for his news, sent him to get some refreshments, and went to a window to watch and wait and wonder about this strange knight who was coming to rescue her.

Lynette and Beaumains rode along toward the castle like two old friends now, and Lynette warned Beaumains about the Red Knight.

"From early morning until noon his strength is as the strength of seven men," she said. "So by all costs you must not challenge him until afternoon."

Soon they came within sight of the Castle Perilous with the red pavilions of the Red Knight pitched all around it. The rosy smoke of campfires drifted in the air. There was the sound of singing and lute playing as the Red Knight's barons entertained themselves. Beyond this busy scene were the waters of the sea, and here and there a small ship with its canvas filled, slipping across the waters which also seemed to have a rosy glow, reflecting the colors of the land.

They rode down the wide track toward the castle

which was lined with trees and lo, they now saw a terrible sight. On every tree a dead knight was hanging from a branch with his shield hanging beside him.

"Oh, no," said Beaumains. "What sort of foul knight would work such villainy?"

"The sad thing," said Lynette, "is that he was not a bad man to start with. He had courtesy as well as strength. But then something happened to him that turned him to these murdering ways."

"It is a wonder that he has endured so long," said Beaumains, "and that no knight from the Round Table has come to deal with him."

By now they had come to a great sycamore tree. On it hung a huge horn made of an elephant's tusk, which the Red Knight had placed there so that any knight coming into his territory would announce his arrival.

"No," said Lynette anxiously, "not now. It is still mid-morning, when his strength is greater than that of seven men. Wait until after noon to blow it."

"Fie, fie," said Beaumains. "Not that old tune again. I will meet him at his utmost might and win my worthship fittingly, or I will die in the field." He went to the tree, picked up the horn, and blew it so loud and long that the blast echoed across the countryside.

The Red Knight heard the call and summoned his barons to help him arm himself. All his armor was blood-red and so were his spurs and his shield. A baron buckled on his red helmet and handed him a red spear. Then they brought forth a red horse and the knight mounted it and rode to a little vale near the castle walls, within sight of everyone both inside and outside the castle.

*   *   *

Beaumains and Lynette rode toward the vale and Lynette said, "Ahead is your enemy, but stop a moment. Up there in that window is the lady you fight for, my sister, the lady Lyonesse."

Beaumains halted his horse for a moment and looked up. There in a wide embrasure he saw a lady who seemed all rose and gold and ivory. The rose and gold were her bodice and gown. The ivory was her pale, lovely face. Pearls looped down from her stiff, pointed headdress and pearls hung from her slender neck. To Beaumains she seemed the most beautiful lady he had ever seen. When she saw him looking up she made a deep curtsy. At this Beaumains lifted his arm in a salute.

The Red Knight cantered toward Beaumains. "Leave off your looking," he shouted. "She is my lady and for her I have done many battles."

"Indeed," Sir Beaumains called back. "Then I fear it is wasted labor for she does not love you and if I did not know she were glad of my coming, I would not be here."

"Ha!" shouted the Red Knight. "No more talking. Make yourself ready."

Beaumains beckoned to Lynette to ride away, off into the meadow nearby. And both he and the Red Knight put their spears in their rests and rushed at each other like boars. They crashed so terribly that both their breastplates cracked and both fell off their horses and lay stunned on the ground for a while. The Red Knight's men watched in wonder. Was it time to go to their lord's rescue?

No. Gradually, the two knights got to their feet. They picked up their shields and their swords. Then they flew at each other, lunging and hacking. First one reeled backward, then the other, and so they fought on and on until it was past noon and both were so out of breath that they stopped, panting and blowing. Then they rushed at each other again.

No one had seen the like before. The armor of the fighters became so hacked and hewn that the watchers could see their naked skin, drooling blood. By mid-afternoon, the fighters came to some sort of unspoken agreement. They sat down a little distance apart and took off their helmets and let the breeze cool their burning faces. Beaumains looked up and saw the lady Lyonesse at her window. The sight restored him enough so that he laced his helmet back on again. He rose, and so did the Red Knight. The lunging, banging, thrusting, and seeking for an opening went on.

The Red Knight raised his arms and with both hands brought his sword down on Beaumains' head so that he went sprawling on the ground. The Red Knight stood over him and it seemed that Beaumains had finally been overwhelmed.

From off to the side came a high, sharp voice which Beaumains knew very well. "Oh, Sir Beaumains, where is all the courage you showed as a kitchen boy? Up, knave, up. My sister, lady Lyonesse, is watching and weeping to see you in such disarray."

At the sound of Lynette's voice, Beaumains pulled himself away from the Red Knight. He rose to his feet and gripped his sword again. In a frenzy he flung himself against his adversary.

Suddenly, it was the Red Knight who was on the ground and Beaumains was standing over him with his sword at his throat. The Red Knight was panting. "I yield me. Mercy, mercy, Sir Knight."

"Why should I show mercy to one who has dealt as you have with those knights hanging from the trees along the avenue? You deserve their fate and worse."

The Red Knight panted. "Let me tell you the reason. Once I loved a lady. Her brother was slain by Sir Launcelot — or perhaps by Sir Gawaine. I promised her I would wage war on all King Arthur's knights whenever, however I could. And so I have done. But now with your mercy I will cease."

Then all of the Red Knight's barons and men came running out onto the field to beg Beaumains to save their lord's life.

"What good will it do you to kill him?" they said. "Let him live to make amends to the families of those he has harmed. And he and we will all become your men and do you homage."

A strange red twilight had fallen over the red lawns and the red pavilions. Beaumains stood a moment in its eerie light, his sword still at the Red Knight's throat.

"This knight has done much harm," he said, "but perhaps he had some reason. For your sakes I will release him, providing that he goes to the lady in the castle and makes amends for all the trouble he has caused her, and wins her forgiveness. When that is done, he and all of you must go to the court of King Arthur and surrender yourselves unto him."

"Sir Knight," said the Red Knight, "all this I promise to do." His barons and knights swore the same.

Beaumains let the Red Knight get to his feet and his men took him to dress his wounds. And Lynette came to do what she could for Sir Beaumains.

That night, they all rested in the pavilions on the field, but the next morning, the Red Knight went to promise his amends to the lady Lyonesse and to win her forgiveness. When that had been done, the Red Knight and his men mounted their horses and rode off to Camelot to surrender themselves and swear their loyalty to King Arthur as they had promised.

The Red Knight and his men made a great sensation when they arrived at Camelot, kneeling before Arthur one after another, saying that they had been sent by Sir Beaumains.

Sir Beaumains, thought King Arthur. Beaumains. He was the youth who had come and asked to serve as a kitchen boy. He had served and then asked Launcelot to knight him. Arthur turned to Launcelot. "This youth must indeed be of some noble blood. Did he tell you his name when you knighted him?"

"He did," said Launcelot, "but I gave my promise that I would not tell the name until he gave me permission."

"Ah well," said Arthur, "I can tell from what you do not say that he is of good stock so we will live with this mystery until the time for its solution." He went back to accepting the homage of the Red Knight's men who knelt before him, one after the other.

Meantime, at the Castle Perilous, Beaumains was asking Lynette if it were not time for him to go into the castle and meet the lady Lyonesse for whom he had battled.

"I think so, yes, Beaumains," said Lynette. Since they were good friends now, she helped him to polish his armor and put it on. She waved as he cantered off.

He rode to the castle and then reined his horse, for lo, the drawbridge was drawn up, and beyond it the gates were closed and men-at-arms were standing on guard.

"Let me enter," he called to the guards. "I have fought for your mistress and freed her from the Red Knight. Let down the bridge so I may enter."

A voice floated down from an upper window. It was not so high as Lynette's but it had something of the perversity of hers. "Not yet, Sir Beaumains, not yet," the lady Lyonesse called to him. "You cannot enter and truly have my love until you have proved yourself a worthy knight."

Sir Beaumains stared at the lady in the window in astonishment. "Proved myself? But surely, lady, I have done something of that."

"Yes, yes," the sweet, perverse voice went on. "You have done much and you have my thanks. But now I think it well that you go your way and come back—oh, a twelvemonth from now, and then I will truly love you."

What was it with these two sisters, Lynette and Lyonesse, that they seemed so determined between them to drive Sir Beaumains to distraction?

He stared up at the lady. Then he wheeled his horse, spurred him, and rode at a gallop away from the castle, up the long way to the forest. There in the forest, for a while he went, as people said in those days, "wood," or "wild wood," meaning crazy.

Perhaps both sisters simply had that curiosity of childhood which is outraged if every question is not answered at once.

At any rate, when the lady Lyonesse finally managed, by one means or another, to learn the true name of Sir Beaumains, she then began bending every effort to bring him back again to Castle Perilous.

As for Sir Beaumains, after he had recovered his wits,

he lived through many adventures. He fought bravely in more than one tournament. He loyally avoided falling in love with a lady who was really Lyonesse in disguise and testing him. And at last he did go back to Castle Perilous.

This time he was welcomed with open arms by lady Lyonesse, and after all the trouble she had caused him it is good to tell that now he found much joy in her.

Sir Beaumains, now revealed as Sir Gareth, and the lady Lyonesse, were married with great ceremony. Arthur and Launcelot and many of the knights of the Round Table came for the festivities. Even Morgawse, Gareth's mother, made her way from the Orkney Isles to the Castle Perilous. And Lynette, who had mocked him for so many miles on their first journey together, mocked him again. "Imagine! A kitchen knave for a brother-in-law," she said. But then she kissed him and they clasped hands and laughed.

VIII.

OF LAUNCELOT AND ELAINE

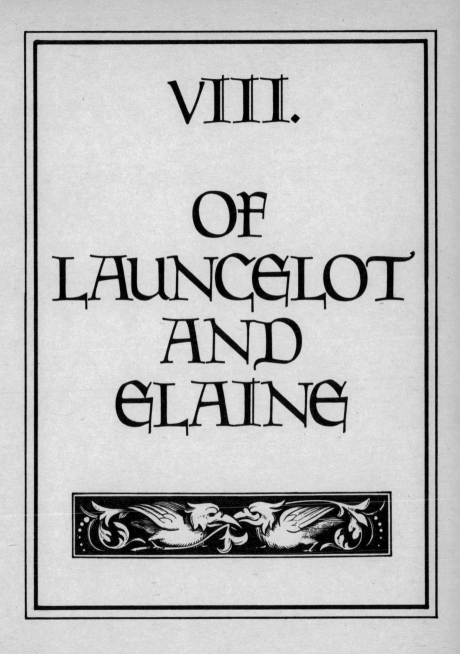

Merlin had foretold it. "One day," he had told Arthur, "I am going to fall in love and that will be the end of me as a wizard."

And so it befell. Merlin met a small, dark girl named Nimue and was so bewitched by her that he taught her all his magic. When Nimue knew all his secrets, or enough of them, she lured him into a cave, blocked the entrance, and made him a prisoner. She visited him now and then when the mood took her, and Merlin was so enamored that he was perfectly content, and Arthur saw him no more.

But of course that was not the end of magic, sometimes working for good, sometimes for ill.

Launcelot ran into a good deal of it, mostly ill, about this time. He was off on another quest for adventure, his love for Guenevere causing a constant restlessness in his blood.

So there he was, riding along, when he came to a village clustered around a castle on a hill.

The villagers recognized him at once.

"Sir Launcelot du Lac," they cried. When he halted they came clamoring about him.

"You are the one," they said. "You can save her. You can work the miracle."

It took a while for Launcelot to find out what they were talking about, but finally he got the story. The daughter of King Pelles who lived in the castle up on the hill had been fearfully magicked some years before so that she had to spend all her days and nights in a vat of boiling water. Various people, including some of King Arthur's knights, had tried to pull her out but without any success.

"You are the one to do it," the villagers said to Launcelot.

He shook his head. He was very sure of himself when he rode into a tourney or against a giant or monster or dragon. But he had no faith at all in being able to do a miracle.

But the villagers would not let him off. Soon he was being led into a great upper room of the castle. In the center of the room was a tub of steaming water, and in the water was a maiden, her face quite rosy from the endless steaming, and her hair a tangle of damp curls piled on top of her head.

Launcelot moved doubtfully toward the tub.

"Just take my hand," said the maiden. "If you are the one, that is all that is needed."

Launcelot put out his hand. The maiden took it. And then, lo—it *was* a miracle. She stood up and stepped out of the tub. Rosy red as she was, Launcelot could see that she was a very pretty girl.

78

Her serving women rushed in with dry clothes for her. And after that there were great outpourings of gratitude from everyone—from the maiden, from King Pelles, and from the villagers. Finally everyone went to church to give thanks and Launcelot was full of gratitude as well, amazed that he had been allowed to work a miracle.

Well, the name of this maiden who was rescued by Launcelot was Elaine, and in later centuries poets would write about her, not always mentioning her long bath in the steaming tub.

She was "Elaine the fair, Elaine the lovable, Elaine the lily maid of Astolat." And in another poem she was called the lady of Shalott, though many people think the name of the town where she lived was Corbin.

At any rate, all the poems tell of how Elaine fell in love with Sir Launcelot. And of course that was exactly what Elaine, daughter of King Pelles, did. She fell totally in love with the knight who had rescued her from her watery misery.

Soon enough she discovered that all his love was given to somebody else. He might admire her and say pleasant things about her beauty (in fact, it was jealousy of that beauty that made the mischievous Morgan le Fay put her into hot water in the first place), but he stayed as placid and distant as an uncle.

Elaine was a single-minded girl. (It was a trait she would pass on to her son.) There she was, rescued from the water and restored to happy, everyday life again, sunshine and dry clothes (which must have been delightful), and fires in the fireplace and good food, but all she wanted was Sir Launcelot.

The nurse who had raised her after her mother's death, Dame Brisen, found her crying in her room, and very soon she learned the reason for the tears.

As it happened, Dame Brisen knew some magic of her own. Nothing like Merlin's or Morgan le Fay's or some of the other great necromancers, but she was clever enough to get her foster-child, Elaine, what she wanted so badly.

That night Launcelot drank wine with King Pelles at dinner. After King Pelles had retired, he drank some more, which was unlike him. Then a messenger came to the castle with a note for him. It was from Guenevere. If Launcelot had not been so befuddled with the wine and whatever Dame Brisen had added to it, he might have wondered a little. In all the months he and Guenevere had loved each other, she had never written to him. Now he was miles from Camelot and how did she know he was in King Pelles' castle? However, here was a note from her, saying that she was staying in a castle nearby. Arthur was off on some business of the kingdom and she was lonely.

All sorts of sunbursts and starbursts went off in Launcelot's mind and he never stopped to think about any of the queerness of it. He ran for his fur mantle. He followed the messenger out of the castle, found his horse, and then rode along with the messenger to a small castle. There he dismounted and followed the messenger who led him to a great dark room where it seemed to Launcelot that his one love, his dear love, was waiting for him.

In the dawn he awoke, feeling sick. He thought, I have betrayed my best friend, Arthur. How can I live with myself after this? I have lost forever the right to be the best knight in the kingdom.

He rose from the bed and went to push aside the great

tapestries that covered the window. He unlatched the window and pushed it open. The cool morning air rushed in and as it flowed about him his enchantment vanished. He looked over to the great bed and saw, not Guenevere, his dear love, but the rosy, curly-haired maiden he had rescued from the tub.

For a moment, he wanted to kill her. His hand reached out, tensing for the sword that would end this wicked creature who had caused him to betray not only Arthur but Guenevere also.

"How could you?" he croaked. "How could you?"

"I love you," Elaine whispered. She began to cry. "I wanted you — and your baby — more than anything."

Naturally Launcelot did not kill this weeping child. He pulled himself together, put on his clothes, and even forced himself to pat her hand before he left the castle.

He roamed about the countryside for many days after that. It seemed ages ago that he had felt especially blessed for being allowed to work the miracle for Elaine. Now he could only think that through his sin he had forfeited everything, Arthur's friendship and Guenevere's love.

Finally, as sinful and unworthy as he felt, he made his way back to Camelot.

He could not help being cheered by the greeting they gave him. And he could not help taking joy in seeing Guenevere again.

Then there came a message to Arthur from Launcelot's father, King Ban of Benwick, asking Arthur's help in a war in France against King Claudas.

"I must go, of course," said Arthur. "Ban was a wonderful help when I was getting control of the Kingdom."

"And I'll go with you, of course," said Launcelot.

"Launcelot," said Arthur, "would you mind very much not going but staying here instead?"

"Staying here? At Camelot?"

"I would like to know that you were the one looking after things while I am away," Arthur said.

Launcelot tried to protest that there were others who might be more suited for the task. But the more he protested the more distressed Arthur became. "Why?" he asked. "Am I really asking too much of you?"

And so it befell that Arthur and many of his knights left for Ban's kingdom in France. Guenevere and Launcelot were left, certainly not alone at Camelot, but with no one in particular paying much attention to what they did.

If Launcelot had not felt that he had already sinned and lost his right to being the best knight in the world, perhaps it would have been a longer time before they came together. But sooner or later it would have happened. And happen it did. It was the first inkling of the shadow that Merlin had seen when he tried to warn Arthur against Guenevere.

For Guenevere and Launcelot there was no hint of a shadow. They had a year of joy.

There was still not a hint of shadow or trouble when Arthur returned at last with his knights from France. He was delighted to be home and full of stories about the battles by which he and King Ban had finally defeated King Claudas.

And then Sir Bors arrived in court, having just been staying with King Pelles. He brought the news that Elaine, the king's daughter, had given birth to a fine son whom she had named Galahad.

Most people at Camelot knew that Launcelot's first name was Galahad. They knew that Launcelot had been at King Pelles' castle and had worked a miracle for his daughter, Elaine, but this was not quite the miracle they had imagined. There was a great deal of quiet laughter in the court. But no laughter at all when Guenevere and Launcelot were finally alone together.

"So," said Guenevere, in a strange voice that hissed through her teeth. "That is why you came to me at last. You said you were giving up your purity for me. Instead...instead—"

Launcelot tried to explain to her how he had been magicked into thinking he was meeting her that night when he had been taken to Elaine. For a long time Guenevere would not listen. But at last she gave in and they clung to each other, and all was well again.

But not for long.

Elaine, the fair, back home in her father's castle in Corbin (as some books have it) or Astolat, or Shalott, or wherever, crooned over her baby, and thought of Sir Launcelot. She brooded because he never came to see her or the child, and then she decided that she would go to him at Camelot, along with the baby.

Her father helped her so that she set off in great state, carrying the baby like an offering. Twenty knights and ten ladies came with her. And of course King Arthur greeted her with all courtesy. Guenevere swallowed hard, and she too made the young woman welcome, though she did not look much at the child. All the knights who were not out questing were quite dazzled by Elaine's beauty and saluted her. Only Launcelot stayed in the shadows and took no part in the greetings.

Elaine's pretty face stiffened. Her whole reason for coming to Camelot had been to win Launcelot to her again somehow. She had her fine clothes. She had their beautiful baby. More than that she had a story about a strange thing that happened that seemed to foretell a wonderful fate for their child. At the feast after his christening, there had been a marvel. A dove had flown into the dining hall, with a little censer of gold in its mouth. While the dove hovered over the tables, a maiden suddenly appeared holding high a tray on which there was a veiled object that shimmered with a light so bright it was impossible to see it clearly.

"Wit well," the maiden had said. "This child, Galahad, shall sit in the Siege Perilous at the Round Table, and he shall win this cup, that no knight else can achieve, the cup that is the Holy Grail or Sangreal." Then the maiden and her tray and the goblet vanished as suddenly as they had appeared. So did the dove with its little censer of gold. All that remained was a sweet smell of spice and incense.

Elaine was anxious to tell Launcelot about all of that, so that he might be pleased with her for having borne a son who evoked such prophecies.

But Launcelot stayed in the shadows and would not go near her or the baby.

Later, Guenevere sought him out. She was feeling terrible pangs of jealousy because of the baby and she said, "I suppose you will go to her tonight."

"Never!" Launcelot almost shouted it.

"I am giving her a room very close to mine," said Guenevere coldly. "I will know if you go to her."

"But it is impossible. I told you. I only went to her before because I was tricked and bewitched."

Guenevere simply turned and walked away.

And then, hard as it may be to believe, it did happen again. Dame Brisen found Elaine crying in her room because Launcelot had not spoken one word to her. Brisen said, "Stop crying, my pretty. Your love will be with you tonight."

Late in the night Dame Brisen went to Launcelot's room and whispered that Guenevere was waiting for him. And he, doped by whatever magic she had fed him, followed her, thinking he was going to his own dear love.

He was back in his own room before dawn and had no notion of how he had been bewitched until Guenevere called him and Elaine to her the next morning.

The queen's face was pale. She was clenching and unclenching her hands. She gasped as she spoke. "False knight. False and traitorous. And in my own court, too!"

Launcelot was bewildered. Then he looked at Elaine who was looking at the floor but smiling self-consciously.

"No, no!" he cried. "Not of my own will. I was bewitched."

"The same story all over again? I was a fool to believe it the first time. Go. Go and I never want to see you again," Guenevere said.

Launcelot tried to speak but his words seemed clotted in his mouth. He stretched out his arms. He fell on his knees. Then, suddenly, he was clutching his head in a sort of frenzy.

He ran across the room to a window that overlooked the courtyard. With one leap he cleared the sill and jumped out onto the ground below. Then he ran like a wild man across the yard and out the gate, over the bridge, and on — to no one knew where.

IX.

MORE OF LAUNCELOT AND ELAINE

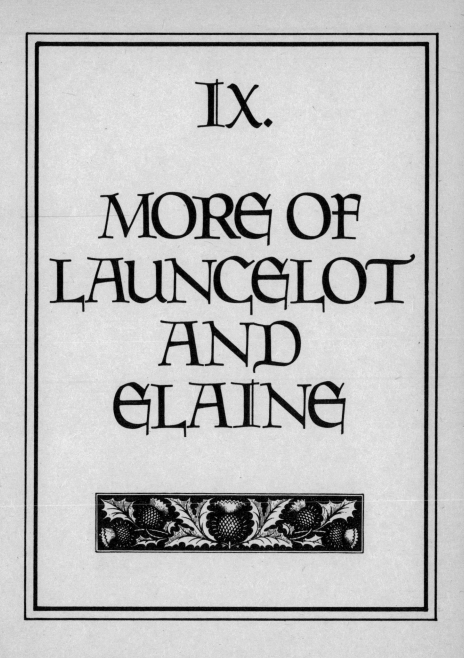

For two years Launcelot ran "wild wood," and no one knew him. Clad in a ragged shirt and breeches, he lived on the fruits and nuts of the forest and drank water from the streams. He grew gaunt and his eyes had a red glare.

In this wild state he had various adventures. One day while he was roaming through a meadow, he came upon the pavilion of a knight. On a tree nearby there hung a shield and two swords. Something about the sight of this knightly equipment stirred a memory in his crazed mind. He reached for one of the swords and when the knight came out of his pavilion the wild man made as if to run at him in combat.

"Hold on now," said the knight gently, "hold on. I am sure that what you really need is some sleep and food and warm clothes." He backed into the pavilion as he spoke. But presently he came out again, this time armed with a sword.

When the poor crazed Launcelot saw him come out so armed he flew at him in his best old style and gave him such a crack over the head that the knight fell to the ground in a swoon. After that, the crazy man ran into the pavilion and jumped into the bed there and pulled the covers around him.

As it happened, the knight's wife had been in the room. When the madman ran in, she fled outside and saw her husband in a sad state.

"Oh dear, oh dear," she cried and hurried to help him. When he finally stood up and she saw that he was not badly hurt she said, "What is going on here?"

The knight, whose name was Bliant, was a good-hearted soul. He shook his head and said, "From the way he handled that sword, that madman once must have been a knight of some reknown. In all charity, I think we must take him back with us to the castle."

Sir Bliant sent his dwarf to the castle with orders for his men to bring more horses and a litter. They arrived and picked up the madman, still asleep in his blanket, and carried him in the litter to the Castle Bliant. There Sir Bliant put him in a small room and had him fettered so he would not roam about, but he also saw to it that he was clothed and fed.

And so many days and nights went by until one day some ruffians overtook Sir Bliant in his own courtyard. He was fighting them off as well as he could, but he was losing ground steadily when the madman in the lower room heard the racket. The madman wrenched and pulled at the fetters that held him. His flesh was torn and his bones twisted, but at last he ran out and with his bare hands he pulled one of the ruffians from his horse. He snatched the ruffian's sword from him and gave him such a whack that he fell to the ground.

Now the other ruffian came riding at the madman but Sir Bliant had recovered enough to rush up and slice off the ruffian's hand just as he was reaching to smite the madman.

After that, both ruffians fled away from the Castle Bliant. And Sir Bliant was so grateful to the madman that he said he would never bind the poor fellow again.

So the crazed Sir Launcelot stayed on some time longer at the castle of Sir Bliant. But even though he was no longer fettered and was well treated, his wits did not return to him.

Then one day it happened that a hunt after a boar went charging across the front lawns of the castle, and poor Launcelot became involved in that. This adventure took him far into the forest, away from the castle. Finally he came face to face with the boar and he was wounded rather badly before he managed to finish off the creature.

A hermit who lived nearby found the bleeding madman and took him to his cave and nursed his wounds. In that cave more days and weeks passed. One day the madman arose from his pallet and again ran out into the woods.

He ran here and he ran there, here and there, until one day he was running down the streets of a little village. He did not know it but this was Corbin (or Astolat or Shalott), the very village that was crowned by the castle of King Pelles, father of Elaine, the fair.

The boys of the village were throwing stones and clumps of mud at him when some of King Pelles' men came to his rescue. They took him from his tormentors and looked at him and by the scars of old wounds they were sure he had once been a man of worth ship. They decided to lodge him in one of the little huts that were built around the castle inside its great walls. Perhaps he might become the court fool.

After that, Sir Launcelot lived in a hut, sleeping on straw, eating food that was thrown in to him through the door, and this not many yards from the castle in which he had once rescued a maiden from a tub of boiling water.

One day there was a celebration at the castle. A nephew of King Pelles had been made a knight and there was much feasting and drinking in his honor. The king also had gifts for everyone, including red robes for all the men. Someone remembered the fool, out in his hut. For a joke, he was brought in and given a red robe. He put it on and suddenly he stood straighter. It was as though the gown, like the sight of a knight's sword, reminded him of something. He walked steadily out of the hall and the laughter was stilled as he passed.

Later that day, one of Elaine's maids came to her and said that a strange man was sleeping by the fountain. Elaine followed the maid and looked at the sleeping man in his red robe. Somehow, this man had stumbled around the castle courtyard for days as the court fool, but after donning the red robe, he had washed his face, combed his hair. Elaine knew him instantly as Sir Launcelot.

Elaine now acted quietly and quite sensibly. She went for her father. When he had recovered from his surprise, everything went very smoothly. Launcelot was taken up into a tower room and put into a comfortable bed and leeches and nurses were summoned to tend him.

But King Pelles was sure he had the true cure for Launcelot's addled brains. In a place of honor in the great hall was a holy relic which King Pelles was sure could work miracles. He ran down the stairs to fetch it and then hurried up again. He stood by Launcelot's bed and took off the silk veil that covered the relic and held it near Launcelot's face. "Open your eyes, Sir Launcelot," he said. "Open your eyes and look and be healed."

And lo, Sir Launcelot opened his eyes, and looked on the relic, and blinked. And after a moment he was looking about with understanding for the first time in many months. He gazed up at King Pelles and at Elaine. "Lord Jesu," he said, "how did I come here? Tell me, in God's name, what does this mean?"

So Elaine and her father told him how he had been running out of his wits, and how Elaine had found him by the fountain in the red robe. Launcelot groaned and asked if everyone knew that the man who had been running mad was Sir Launcelot.

Elaine and her father soothed him, telling him truly that only they and the ones who were attending him knew his identity.

He lay recovering for several days. When Elaine came in to see how he fared, he beckoned her to him.

"Lady," he said, "there is no need to rehearse the harm you have done me, twice deceiving me into terrible betrayals of my true love. But I have done wrong as well. Once I was ready to draw my sword against you. Now I would ask a boon. I can never return to Camelot or Arthur's court. Do you think your father can provide me with some place in this countryside where I may live out my days?"

"Oh, Launcelot, Launcelot," cried Elaine. "You will stay and we will live together with our child and be happy forever and all will be as it should be."

Launcelot closed his eyes against the sight of her happiness which was so different from what he felt. But he had made up his mind and from now on he would be as gentle and kind as possible.

Elaine made her request of her father and King Pelles was delighted to offer one of his castles to Launcelot and Elaine. It was a very good one, on an island surrounded by pleasant water. He also offered a number of ladies-in-waiting and knights and servants to make everything easy for them.

Elaine was almost dizzy with delight. "We will call the castle the Joyous Isle," she said, as she and Launcelot rode toward it. And Launcelot bowed his head in agreement.

But it was at this time, because he wanted no one to know his true name, that he began to call himself Le Chevalier Mal Fait, — The Knight Who Had Done Wrong, or the Badly Made Knight, depending on how one translates the French.

For a long time Launcelot lived with Elaine in the castle she called Joyous Isle. He saw how hard she tried to make him content and not to ask too much of him and so he tried also to be kindly and courteous. But every day he went up to one of the towers and looked toward Camelot where Guenevere and King Arthur were, and the tears came to his eyes in spite of himself.

Still he was a knight, and he could not rest forever without using his knightly skills.

He heard of a tourney that was taking place not many

miles from the Joyous Isle. He sent a messenger to invite all the knights to another tourney to joust with Le Chevalier Mal Fait.

They came by the dozens. Later, some said by the hundreds. One after the other they rode out against Le Chevalier Mal Fait and were unhorsed and beaten, but no one was really hurt or killed. And all wondered who this strange knight could be. But even through all the feasting that followed the tourney no one had a clue as to who he was.

Later, two more knights came and when the first of them challenged Launcelot, he rode forth as always and fought with that knight for more than two hours. Then the strange knight suddenly held back his spear and said, "Tell me your name."

"My name is Le Chevalier Mal Fait," said Launcelot. "What is yours?"

The other said, "My name is Sir Percival, son of King Pellinore, brother of Sir Aglovale."

When he heard that, Launcelot threw his spear to the ground and leaped off his horse, and ran to the other knight.

"Why am I fighting with a knight of the Round Table, a knight who was so long my fellow?"

Sir Percival was bewildered. "Who are you really?" he asked. "Either tell me or unlace your helmet so that I may see you."

Sir Launcelot said, "Truly, I am Sir Launcelot du Lac, son of King Ban of Benwick." Then he lifted his helm so that Percival could see that it was indeed so.

"Launcelot!" cried Percival. "To think that I should be fighting you when we have all been searching for you for these two years. And over there, waiting his turn—

do you know who that is? Sir Ector de Maris, your brother."

Launcelot ran to Sir Ector and threw his arms around him. "Brother," he cried.

After that, all three talked at once for quite a while as Percival and Ector tried to learn where Launcelot had been and what he had been doing through the years he had been gone from Camelot.

Then Ector said, "And now, of course, you are coming back with us."

"How can I?" said Launcelot. "The queen told me never to come there again."

"She has changed her mind since then," said Sir Ector. "She has had half the knights of the Round Table out searching for you during the last years."

"Arthur grieves for you too. The Round Table is not the same without you," said Percival.

"Guenevere has been looking for me?" asked Launcelot.

"We told you. At one time there must have been a hundred of us out, riding here and there, looking for some sign of you."

Launcelot was silent a moment. Then he said, "I have settled here with Elaine. She loves me. She depends on me."

"And you love her?" asked Percival.

Launcelot said, "She has been trying very hard to make up for what she did."

"Yes, well," said Percival, "you have some obligations to Arthur too. You are his best knight who swore to serve him always."

"Obligations to Guenevere too," said Ector. "She blames herself terribly for your disappearance, and talks of you constantly."

A while later Elaine said, "You will come back someday?"

Launcelot hardly knew what he was saying. "Yes, I will come back someday."

"And our child, Galahad," said Elaine. "When the time comes you will surely be the one to knight him?"

"To knight him?" The day when the boy would be old enough to be knighted seemed very far away to Launcelot.

Elaine said, "I told you of the miracle at his christening. How a maiden brought in the Sangreal and prophesied that our son would sit at the Round Table in the Siege Perilous where none but the purest knight of all might sit. And that one day he would win the Sangreal."

"Yes, yes," said Launcelot. He had almost forgotten the story Elaine had told him and did not know how much of it he believed anyway. Besides his thoughts were already in Camelot.

And then, before too many days had passed, he was really there. Arthur was holding his hands and shaking them as if he would never let go. Guenevere was glowing at him like the sun. And there was great rejoicing and feasting and music at Camelot with Launcelot's return.

X.

OF SIR GALAHAD

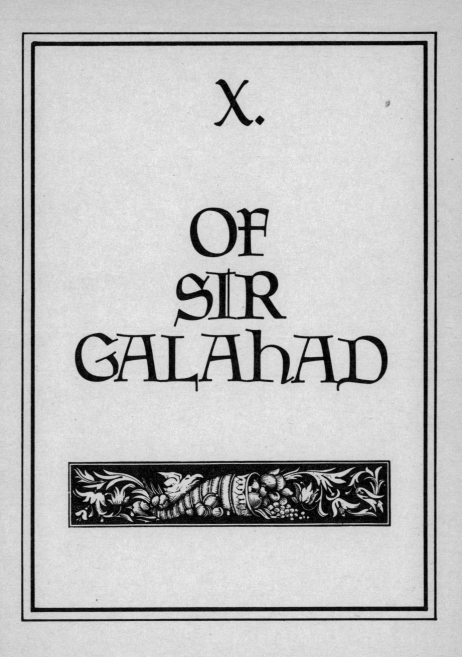

They were preparing for another feast of the Pentecost at Camelot. The great Round Table was being polished. All the seats were being dusted, and the knights' names on them, in gold letters, were being shined. Pages were bringing in fresh rushes and spreading them across the floor to make everything new and sweet for the springtime.

By now there had been a goodly number of such Pentecostal feasts at Camelot. Arthur had been king of England for some twenty years or more. And the knights who had sworn to the vows of the Round Table —to right wrongs and help those in need—had done a great deal to make England a happier place. There were far fewer robbers and murderers roaming the highways and byways these days, far fewer giants and monsters and ogres kidnapping maidens or torturing children, far fewer cruel knights riding down upon innocent men to skewer them just for the fun of it.

Still there were adventures to be had, and quests to

follow and young men eager to be one of King Arthur's knights of the Round Table.

This year, on the day before the great feast, a lady rode into the courtyard at Camelot, asking for Sir Launcelot. When he was found and came to her, she said, "Sir, I salute you in the name of King Pelles and beg you to come with me on an urgent errand in a nearby forest."

"King Pelles? Elaine's father?" asked Launcelot. "What does he want of me?"

"Come with me," said the lady.

So Launcelot went for his armor and his horse and soon he joined the lady and they rode off together.

They came to the forest and rode along through the trees until they came to a nunnery. There the lady reined her horse and told him to dismount. "This is the place," she said.

Launcelot had slid down from his horse but was still wondering when a procession of nuns came out of the courtyard. Then the columns of nuns parted and Launcelot saw they were escorting a fair young man.

"Sir," said the Abbess of the nunnery, "we bring you this young man whom we have been nourishing and teaching and beg you to make him a knight."

Launcelot looked at the lad and thought he had never seen anyone so comely. "Is this by his own desire?" he asked.

The youth nodded. "Oh, sir, it is," he said. "And I would receive my knighthood from none other than you."

It was all rather strange. But Launcelot was so bemused by the smiling, nodding, waiting nuns, and by the beauty of the eager young man that he agreed.

And so it befell that Sir Launcelot knighted his own

son, Galahad, grandson of King Pelles, whom Elaine had sent to the nuns for teaching. After that, he returned to Camelot in time for the feast of Pentecost.

And this was the feast at which were more wonders than any had seen in a long time, wonders that ushered in a new era of the Round Table.

The first wonder occurred before they even sat down at the great table. One of the king's squires came hurrying to Arthur.

"Sir, a strange and marvelous thing! On the river just beyond the castle walls, a great red marble stone seems to float on the water, and in the stone is thrust a sword."

Arthur stared a moment and shook his head as if to clear it. There had been a sword in a stone a long, long time ago, in a churchyard, and the one who had drawn it had been proved rightwise King of England. Now there was another sword in a stone?

He said to his assembled knights, "Perhaps we should go see this marvel."

The whole company went down to the river and indeed there was a great red stone, and in it was thrust a sword. The hilt of the sword was crusted with jewels and it seemed there was lettering as well.

One of the knights waded out to the stone and read out what was written on the hilt.

No man shall take me hence but only he who shall be the best knight in the world.

"Launcelot," said Arthur, "this sword must be yours. Go draw it out."

But Launcelot had a strange premonition that this was not for him and that some curious new adventure was impending.

"Oh come on, come on," said Arthur. Then he turned

103

to Gawaine. "You give it a try," he said. And Gawaine obediently went out to the stone and pulled at the hilt of the sword but he could not move it.

"Please, Launcelot," said Arthur. And this time Launcelot sighed and went out into the water and gave a sharp tug at the sword, but he could not move it either. After that, other knights tried their luck with no success.

Then King Arthur said, "This seems a marvel that must wait a bit for its fulfillment. Let us go back now to the castle."

Back at the castle, each knight took his place in the siege lettered with his name. Then came the next surprise.

In walked an old man, leading a youth in armor, although the young man had no shield and the scabbard at his side had no sword in it.

The old man went up to King Arthur and said, "I bring you a new knight — one of a noble lineage who will confer new honor to your Round Table."

"Welcome, indeed," said the king to the youth. Then he waved a hand. "I am sure there is an empty seat somewhere there on the far side of the table."

But the old man led the youth straight to the seat that was called the Siege Perilous and which was kept veiled.

Standing by that seat, the old man took off the youth's armor and put on him a red cloak trimmed in ermine. Then he pulled back the silk that veiled the Siege Perilous and lo, there was new gold lettering that spelled out the name, *Sir Galahad*.

The youth in the red furred cloak took the seat and all the knights around the table stared. This was the seat that meant death to anyone who was not worthy to sit in it. But there sat the fair young man, very quietly and calmly.

Sir Launcelot looked at the youth and recognized the lad he had knighted the day before — his own son, Sir Galahad. He felt a great happiness and pride as he saw him sitting there in the Siege Perilous. At the same time, he felt a strange sinking away inside himself. He felt himself growing old.

After that, a great many things happened, one after the other, and so quickly that they almost blurred in everyone's minds. Was it before or after the feast that everyone went back to the river again and the new young knight, Galahad, was given the opportunity to pull the sword from the stone?

Whenever, before or after, Galahad drew the sword forth easily, just as once, long ago, Arthur had drawn a sword from a stone in a churchyard.

The crowd murmured and buzzed. Was this young lad, still downy-cheeked, indeed the best knight in the world?

The young knight, Galahad, slipped the sword into the scabbard by his side, where it seemed perfectly at home. And there was more murmuring and buzzing.

But then everybody went back to the great hall and when they had gathered around the Round Table, lo, there was another marvel.

A crash of thunder echoed through the hall. There was a flash of lightning, and then a vision floated over the table. It was something shaped like a goblet, but veiled in white silk. It floated and glowed and shimmered above the table like some magical moon. All the while it hovered there, almost too bright to look at; the air was perfumed with the sweetest fragrance and there was a sense of music somewhere. Everyone around the table stared in stunned surprise. Then the vision floated off, away, and was gone.

"The Holy Grail," whispered Arthur. "The Sangreal."

The knights looked at each other, awed at what they had been allowed to witness. The very cup from which Jesus had drunk at the Last Supper.

Then Gawaine said, "But it was veiled." He stood. Big and burly Gawaine, who had never been noted for his piety, said, "I would see it unveiled—the Sangreal itself in all its glory. Then would I be willing to die. And now I make a vow. I shall go questing to see that sight and find the Holy Grail on whatever altar it rests."

Gaheris, Gawaine's brother, leaped to his feet. "I too would see the Holy Grail. I too will go questing for it." Agravaine jumped up. "I too. I vow it."

Suddenly, all the knights at the Table were on their feet, making the vow. A kind of hysteria had come over them all—all except Arthur.

"No," he said, shaking his head. "No."

It was strange. He was the one who had once had the vision of questing to right wrongs and help the helpless. But now, when Gawaine (of all people) had a vision of questing after the earth's holiest object, he felt it wrong and foolish. In his mind's eye, he saw all the knights riding off to the ends of the earth on a hopeless chase. He saw them injured and killed in their search and finally an end to his Round Table.

"Wait!" he called, standing up. "Listen! Think a moment. Isn't it said that only those who are absolutely pure in heart and altogether without sin can look upon the Sangreal unveiled?"

The knight Galahad, his new sword in his scabbard,

stood quietly amidst the tumult and said nothing.

But the fever had taken over all the other knights. They paid no attention to what Arthur said and raised their goblets to toast their new vows.

"We will find the Holy Grail," they said. "See it plain! Then all sins will be forgiven."

Gawaine shouted, "I leave in the morning!" At once, a dozen other knights were shouting that they too would be leaving at dawn.

As it turned out, Arthur was right in his fears about this particular quest. His knights rode off in all directions and a great many strange things happened to them. This was the time when magic boats seemed to appear now and then and waft people around for quite a while to no particular purpose. Launcelot found himself on such a boat once with his son Galahad. Percival and Bors were on another one for quite a while, along with a dead lady.

The adventures all the knights had on these quests after the Sangreal were uncanny. Not like the head-on fights of the past.

One night Sir Launcelot found himself at the entrance of a chapel. Looking inside, he saw what had to be the Sangreal on the altar, shimmering in its glory. He smelled the sweet odors that always surrounded it. He heard the heavenly music. He moved to step inside, and invisible forces stopped him and threw him to the ground. For a long time he lay senseless there until a hermit came and found him and took him to his dwelling and nursed him back to health. Launcelot was not a man without sin.

His son, Galahad, had many curious adventures as he went questing after the grail. He found a white shield, marked with a red cross, and it turned out that he was the only one who could carry it without harm.

He rescued a group of maidens who were being held prisoner in a castle and he punished their captors without really injuring any of them. In fact, through all of his adventures, though he fought with many challengers, Galahad never killed anyone.

He traveled awhile with Sir Percival and Sir Bors, and they were with him when they finally came to a chapel in a far country — and again they saw the Sangreal.

It was two years and more before Sir Bors came back to Camelot with the news that of all three of them, Sir Galahad was the only one who had been allowed to touch and lift the Sangreal.

It seemed strange to some at Camelot, who knew how this youth had been born of Elaine's deceit and magic, that he should be the one to grow to manhood with no stain of sin on him. But there it was. He had killed no one. Never lied or cheated or foresworn anyone. To some, it seemed he had never loved anyone either, only the vision of the Grail. However it was, in this purity, he had been given the supreme reward.

Then Sir Bors told the end of the story. After touching the Grail, Galahad had fallen to his knees before the altar and given up his spirit. Sir Bors had seen the angels descend into the chapel and then rise again taking Galahad's soul to heaven. Sir Bors had seen another troop of angels descending and they had picked up the Sangreal and Galahad's spear and these also they carried upward into heaven.

And so, with Galahad's death, and the ascension of the Sangreal to heaven, there came an end to the questing for the Holy Grail on earth.

XI.

OF THE DEATH OF ARTHUR

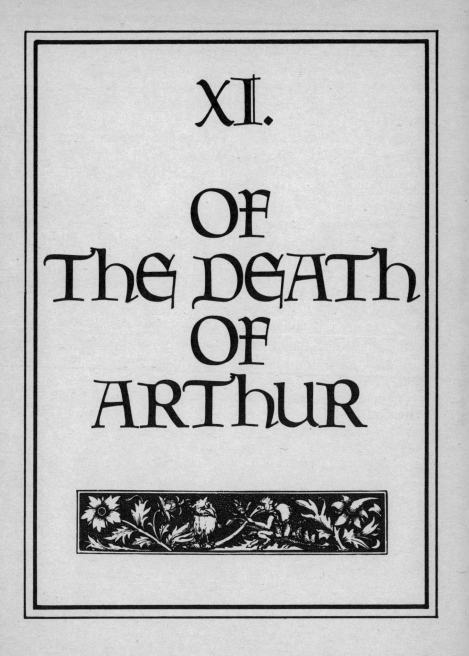

We come now to that long shadow that Merlin had seen following Guenevere.

We come also to the consequences of Merlin's forgetting, long, long ago, to tell Arthur that Morgawse was his half-sister.

One was a shadow on Guenevere. One a shadow on Arthur. But when the two shadows came together there was darkness that eclipsed the sun that had shone for so long over the Round Table at Camelot.

Because both Guenevere and Launcelot loved Arthur dearly he was able to know that they loved each other and also not to know it, so that everything could go along happily with no one making a fuss.

But then came Mordred, Arthur's son by Morgawse. He was made a knight by Arthur himself and Arthur treated him as a well-loved son.

But Mordred could not love his father. He knew the whole story of May day, and how he had been one of the boy babies loaded on to a ship and taken off to sea to perish. He knew he had been the chief cause of this dreadful deed. And in the years after Morgawse found him, she said nothing to make him forgive his father.

And so Mordred came to the Round Table a pale, thin young man, and he did a certain amount of jousting and went on various quests and took part in a few adventures. But all that was only by-the-way to him. What he really wanted to do was punish the father who had tried to kill him when he was an infant.

He went about watching, watching, and looking for his opportunity.

Finally the answer came to him and it was perfectly simple.

There was that long, long love between Guenevere and Launcelot that everyone knew about and pretended not to know. Suppose he made everyone stop pretending. Arthur would be forced to deal out the various punishments, for Arthur now was known far and wide as the king who had brought law and justice to England. He would have to have his wife, Guenevere, burned as an adulteress. Launcelot would have to be banished at the very least.

A thin smiled curved Mordred's lips as he thought about it. He would not be killing his father. Merely breaking his heart.

He had a hard time convincing his half-brothers to go along with him. Morgawse's four sons by King Lot — Gawaine, Gaheris, Agravaine, and Gareth—were strong on family loyalty and Mordred was their youngest brother. Still they were not eager to stir up the waters as he proposed. In the end, only Agravaine was willing to conspire with Mordred.

What they did was arrange for Arthur to go off on a

boar hunt. With Arthur gone, they merely waited until Sir Launcelot went, as so often before, to Guenevere's chambers.

Mordred and Agravaine had gathered twelve other knights around them. When they knew that Launcelot had gone to the queen, they came thundering to the door.

"Open!" they called. "Open in the king's name."

Guenevere and Launcelot looked at each other. He had come to her without his armor.

"Is there any armor here?" he asked.

She shook her head.

The pounding was like to deafen them. Because the door was built double thick, with the boards going crosswise one way and then crosswise the other, there was no way that those outside could break it down. Still they had to be answered.

Launcelot went to the door and opened it a crack. The knight pressing closest to the door at that point was fairly pushed in further. Launcelot gave him a blow, dragged him inside, crashed the door shut after him, and then finished him off with his own sword.

Praying God to forgive him, Launcelot now dressed himself in the dead knight's armor and opened the door and took on all the rest of the knights who were clamoring there.

One by one, he killed them all.

Except Mordred.

Some days before, Arthur had confessed to Launcelot his sin against Mordred when he was just an infant. He had won Launcelot's promise that he would never slay Mordred, no matter what.

But now, with twelve knights killed at the queen's

chamber door, it had to be known that Sir Launcelot had been inside with the queen. There was no way to keep it still.

Arthur had to face it, out in the open. And since he had talked so much of justice and made so much of the need for law, he had no choice but to condemn Guenevere to be burned for adultery.

Everything was made ready. The pyre for the burning was prepared. Guenevere, no longer robed in a queen's silks and velvets, was dressed in a rough shift. There were no pearls looped into her hair, no headdress with filmy veil. Her hair hung in two braids over her shoulders. A priest walked beside her. And Arthur only prayed that Launcelot would come soon to rescue the queen.

And of course Launcelot did come, from wherever he had been. He rode in wildly at the last moment, slashing about him with his terrible sword. Then as one knight after another fell before him, he came and snatched Guenevere from the platform where she was awaiting her doom. He put her on his horse before him and rode swiftly away, taking her to the castle that was called Joyous Gard. (Perhaps this was the same castle that Elaine had once named Joyous Isle. It may have been, for she was no longer there. She had long since joined the nunnery where she had taken young Galahad for his teaching.)

Arthur breathed a sigh of relief. Launcelot had rescued the queen. She was safe.

Then came Mordred and Agravaine with awful tidings. Among the knights slain by Launcelot as he made his wild ride to rescue Guenevere had been their dear brothers, Gareth and Gaheris. And they had been unarmed!

"This cannot go unavenged," said Mordred. And Arthur, weeping for his nephews, Gareth and Gaheris, knew that it could not.

Now even Gawaine, the oldest of the Orkney Isles brothers, was against Launcelot. "If he had not taken them unarmed."

"It is so unlike Launcelot," said Arthur. "He was always sparing of those unarmed."

"Well, this time he was not," said Mordred. "And he must be brought to justice."

So Arthur and his knights had to ride and lay siege to the castle where Launcelot had taken Guenevere.

Very soon the siege settled into a stalemate since Launcelot would not come out to fight against any of his old companions.

There was little joy within the castle called Joyous Gard either, for Launcelot was sick at heart that he had killed Gareth and Gaheris. (Gareth, you may remember, was the lad he had knighted when he was still serving as a kitchen boy.) He had not recognized either of them in his rush to the queen. He had not seen they were unhelmeted. Too much had happened too soon.

And so, though Launcelot and Guenevere were together now as once they might have dreamed of being, they sat sadly before the fire and wondered how this sad state could ever be altered.

It ended, finally, when the Pope himself sent word from Rome that the queen should be pardoned and the king should take her back to him. The archbishop, troubled by the long siege, had written to the Pope to ask for his intervention and it had been arranged in this way. Sir Launcelot should return the queen to her castle, and after that, he should be banished from England.

Launcelot took Guenevere back to Camelot in fine, brave style. She had ladies-in-waiting attending her, all dressed in green velvet picked out with gold. A hundred knights rode with them, and they too were in green velvet. Launcelot and Guenevere were clothed in dazzling new outfits of white trimmed with gold tissue.

So they came before King Arthur and knelt before him.

There were tears in Arthur's eyes as he greeted the two he loved most in the world. He would have pardoned them both, and had them both back beside him as once they had been if it had been his choice alone.

But Sir Gawaine was on one side of him and Sir Mordred on the other. Sir Gawaine's face was set and hard as he insisted on Launcelot's full punishment for killing Gareth and Gaheris as he had. Sir Mordred's face was tight and faintly smiling as he insisted on whatever would most hurt Arthur.

Arthur raised Guenevere from her knees and kissed her. But he dared not raise Launcelot.

"Justice must be done," said Gawaine grimly. And Mordred nodded.

So Launcelot rose and kissed Arthur's hand and then he kissed Guenevere's. He looked in both their eyes and nodded a little. Then he turned and walked with a quiet step all down the length of the hall and out into the courtyard.

After that Launcelot and all his knights departed from Camelot. But because Launcelot had been banished, he had to travel all the miles to the sea on foot, walking in the middle of the road, and holding a crucifix, and then take ship for France. Because he was Launcelot, he did it without a murmur, and came to the shore and went aboard the ship By and by he was in France and in the castle at Benwick that had been his father's.

And now, all should have been at peace, or at least quiet. But Sir Mordred and Sir Gawaine would not have it so. "He must be made to pay for his sin in killing Gareth and Gaheris unarmed," Gawaine said over and over. And Mordred fingered his sword and spoke quietly of other reasons why Launcelot should not be left in exile undisturbed.

How did these two win such power over Arthur? He was a king who had once been able to turn a whole country around and send its knights out to right wrongs and help the helpless. Now he seemed helpless under their prodding.

But of course it was more than the two of them. Arthur suffered under his own guilt, the shadow that came from the days when he had loved Morgawse, and later, when he had allowed the terrible May day command. And he bowed to the son he had once tried to destroy.

So Arthur's war with Launcelot went on. He and his knights went to France and camped before the castle at Benwick, and every day Gawaine sent a challenge to Launcelot to come out and fight him. Every day Launcelot refused to fight his old friend.

At home in England, Arthur had left Mordred in charge, as a sort of regent. Mordred was the heir to the throne, after all.

Left in power, Mordred now began to go quite mad. So far he had arranged everything for his father's humiliation and sorrow so well that he began to think there was nothing he could not manage.

He sent word to Guenevere that Arthur had been

defeated and killed in the siege against Launcelot.

Guenevere was still trying to take in such tidings, her eyes wide and her face in her hands, when young Mordred came to her.

He told her that since Arthur was dead he was soon to be proclaimed king of England and crowned at Canterbury. And after that, he would take her as his wife.

Guenevere stared at him—at his white, smiling face. Now she saw he was mad and she thought how to deal with it.

Finally she nodded. "Very well," she said, "but if I am to be married, there are various things I need. I would like to go to London."

Mordred considered. Should he allow this or not? Finally he said, "You may go."

Guenevere went with all haste, with her ladies, and with all the knights who had always served her. When she arrived in London, she went at once to the Tower. Then she ordered her people to bring in every sort of provision against a long siege. After that she went within and shut herself in, prepared for anything but to see Mordred again.

Of course Mordred set up a siege against the Tower to bring the queen out. He would not stop even when the archbishop himself came and warned him. "You cannot wed your father's wife," the archbishop said. "Leave off this mad action or else I shall curse you with book and bell and candle."

"Go ahead," said Mordred. He was now quite beside himself and was getting cannons with which to shell the Tower. He was also getting allies from the north to join his forces as he attacked the Tower, and there were many who came, believing him to be the new king.

Word finally got to France. Arthur heard that he had been pronounced dead. That Mordred had proclaimed himself king and was about to marry Guenevere.

He and his men left the siege at Benwick within the hour, made their way to the coast, and took ship for England.

The news was a little longer in reaching Launcelot within the castle at Benwick. As soon as he heard it, he and his men were also on their way. But a storm came up as they reached the coast, and they were forced to wait, frantic, until it died down enough for them to set sail.

In England, Arthur and his men met Mordred and his men in one battle after another. The fortunes of war went forth. Then Arthur sent word to his son that they should speak together of a truce.

Mordred agreed to a meeting, on the condition that no knight should raise a sword during the talk.

So Arthur came to Mordred down a long line of knights. And he was beginning to speak quietly to Mordred when lo, a small snake came and bit one knight on the ankle. The knight raised his sword to smite the snake.

In an instant all Mordred's men were raising their swords and rushing upon Arthur's knights, and the battle was on again. It raged in fury all that day and as night fell Arthur saw hundreds of his knights lying dead around him.

He stood in the dark, feeling old and weary. It seemed to him that nothing he had tried for or dreamed of had come to anything. All he had achieved was more death.

Now, for the first time, Arthur went a little crazy. He took his sword and sought out his own son, Mordred.

They raised their swords against each other and Arthur killed Mordred but before he fell Mordred had given Arthur a fatal blow.

Arthur staggered back to his pavilion and lay on his bed.

One of his knights, Sir Bedivere, came to him and knelt by him weeping. "Sire, what can I do for you?" he asked.

"Stop weeping," said Arthur. "There is my sword, Excalibur. Take it to the lake and throw it in. Then come back to me and tell me when you have done so."

Sir Bedivere took the sword and went with it to the lake but when he came to the shore it seemed a pity to throw away such a beautiful weapon. He hid it under a bush and came back to Arthur in his tent.

"You did as I asked you?" said Arthur. "And what did you see at the lake?"

"At the lake? Why nothing, sir, only the waves lapping."

Arthur roused himself a little. "Bedivere, please! Let us have no more of this untruth and betrayal. Take my sword as I told you or I shall never die in peace."

Then Sir Bedivere went back to where he had left the sword. Now he lifted it high and threw it out into the lake. Then he saw an arm, draped in silk, rise out of the lake and grasp the sword and shake it three times before it disappeared into the water.

After this, Bedivere returned to the King and told him about the mysterious arm.

"Ah," sighed the king. "I thank you. Now it is done, and I may go." He closed his eyes and soon thereafter he died.

EPILOGUE

There are various stories about what happened next. Some chroniclers say that Arthur did not really die but that three queens, led by Morgan le Fay, came and carried him to a barge and then rowed him to a magic island called Avalon, where no one ever died. There, these chroniclers say, Arthur lives to this day.

There are others who tell of the grave where he was buried but they also tell of the words written on the tombstone: *Hic jacet Arthurus Rex quondam rex que futurus...*

The Latin, translated, means "Here lies King Arthur, once and future king." Meaning again, that someday the king who had done so much for England would return.

And what of Guenevere and Launcelot?

By the time Launcelot and his men arrived in England, Arthur was dead, Mordred was dead, Sir Gawaine had died in battle, and Guenevere had fled from the Tower to a convent.

Launcelot prayed at the tomb of Sir Gawaine, and sick at heart over the death of Arthur, he finally made his way to the convent.

Guenevere saw him at the end of a long gallery and swooned. And even after she was revived, she would not go to see him. So Launcelot went on his way again.

Later he heard that Guenevere had died in the convent.

Launcelot himself went to a monastery and became a man of God before he too died.

And so the great years of King Arthur's reign came to an end. And with the end of the reign came the end of those he had loved and who had loved him.

But still some glory remained in the land. There was a memory of the time when knights rode forth to right wrongs, to help the helpless, to live pure and speak true. The shadows of mortal sin had fallen across the glory and put the sunlight out. But the sun always rises again, and with it, a new hope for overcoming yesterday's mistakes. And perhaps always the promise: Arthur — the once and future king.